2/24

ALSO BY CYNTHIA ZARIN

POEMS

The Swordfish Tooth
Fire Lyric
The Watercourse
The Ada Poems
Orbit
Next Day: New and Selected Poems

NONFICTION

An Enlarged Heart: A Personal History
Two Cities

CHILDREN'S BOOKS

Rose and Sebastian
What Do You See When You Shut Your Eyes?
Wallace Hoskins, the Boy Who Grew Down
Albert, the Dog Who Liked to Ride in Taxis
Saints Among the Animals

INVERNO

INVERNO

CYNTHIA ZARIN

FARRAR, STRAUS AND GIROUX
New York

Farrar, Straus and Giroux
120 Broadway, New York 10271

Printed in the United States of America
First edition, 2024

Owing to limitations of space, all acknowledgments for permission to reprint
previously published material can be found on page 134.

Snowflake ornament from Popcic / Shutterstock.com.

Library of Congress Cataloging-in-Publication Data
Names: Zarin, Cynthia, author.
Title: Inverno / Cynthia Zarin.
Description: First edition. | New York : Farrar, Straus and Giroux, 2024. |
Identifiers: LCCN 2023031244 | ISBN 9780374610135 (hardback)
Subjects: LCGFT: Romance fiction. | Novels.
Classification: LCC PS3576.A69 I58 2024 | DDC 811/.54—dc23/eng/20230713
LC record available at https://lccn.loc.gov/2023031244

Designed by Patrice Sheridan

Our books may be purchased in bulk for promotional, educational, or business
use. Please contact your local bookseller or the Macmillan Corporate and
Premium Sales Department at 1-800-221-7945, extension 5442, or by email at
MacmillanSpecialMarkets@macmillan.com.

www.fsgbooks.com
Follow us on social media at @fsgbooks

1   3   5   7   9   10   8   6   4   2

FOR JANE

Caminar Sopra 'l giaccio, e à passo lento
Per timor di cader gersene intenti;
Gir forte Sdruzziolar, cader à terra
Di nuove ir Sopra 'l giaccio e correr forte
Sin ch' il giaccio si rompe, e si disserra;
Sentir uscir dalle ferrate porte
Sirocco Borea, e tutti i Venti in guerra
Quest' é 'l verno, mà tal, che gioja apporte.

Slowly we pick our way across
the ice for fear of falling;
turnabout, slip and crash,
rise and run across the ice once more
before it cracks and breaks apart;
hearing through the iron gates
the battling north, south,
and all the other winds—
this is winter, these the joys it brings.

—ANTONIO VIVALDI, "L'INVERNO,"
LE QUATTRO STAGIONI

INVERNO

SHE WOKE TOO EARLY. She'd gone to sleep late and woke during the night. Bars of light fell where the Chinese rug was frayed. The tassel at the edge of the gray curtain caught the glare like a rose in the sweep of a headlight. She had come home later than planned and had left her bag in the middle of the floor. Sometime in the early morning, a nightmare. She'd gone to shut the light off in the hall, but in her dream the light switch was illuminated; it was blue. She knew not to touch it. Between waking and sleep it wasn't clear whether the door to the hall opened from the bedroom in the house where she lived now, where she'd lived for many years and had fallen asleep, the green room where across from the bed over the mantel was a print of a bird in a clutch of flowers, or was it the door from her childhood room that led into a room that was shared by her brothers? Upstairs the children were asleep, dreaming. Were the sleeping children her brothers, sleeping mouths open, one blond, one black-haired, like children in a fairy tale? Or were they her own children, knock-kneed even in sleep, ready to wake in an instant, to play the game saved for when a nightmare sent them bolt upright: What was your dream?

Give it to me. She put out her hand. "There," she said, "I have it." She patted her pocket. George liked her to stroke his eyelids, a forefinger to the ridge of his cheekbone, a tiny scallop shell. No, it was the green room.

*

Caroline is standing by the north ball fields in Central Park in the snow. It is February. There is some kind of construction going on—or it was going on—the big yellow trucks have stalled, but still, she has had to circumvent them. She is walking southeast, toward Seventy-Ninth Street, through the park. It is freezing. The sky is pewter. The iron railings are so cold that she's sure if she took her hand out of her glove and touched one, her finger would freeze in place. As it is, she's stuck. Snow is drifting over her fur-lined boots. She is wearing a sheepskin coat and a fox-fur hat. Her aunt had given it to her. She said, when Caroline arrived at her door wearing the hat, "See, I was going to give it to the Guild for the Blind but then I thought, Caroline will wear it." She is wearing it in the snow as she walks east and waits for Alastair to call her back on her cell phone, which she has set on vibrate and put inside her glove.

When Caroline first began to speak to Alastair on the phone thirty years ago, there were two ways to do it. There was a rotary phone in her tiny apartment that sat in a cradle like a blackened crab. When you wanted to make a call, or the phone rang, you picked up the receiver, and cradled it under your chin, placing one end by your ear and the other next to your mouth. Can I express the intimacy of this relationship, with the telephone? The round earpiece and the mouthpiece, identical, were perforated with tiny holes through which the sound entered and departed. The receiver was connected to the cradle by a black spiral cord. The cords could be different lengths. If the telephone had a long cord, you could walk around with the phone; if it was a short cord, you sat next to it while you spoke. In either case, you were tethered. The phone was attached to the wall at a special outlet, called a "telephone jack." The plug was a little square of clear plastic. The round plastic dial of the telephone looked like a clockface. Like a clockface, numbers circled the dial. There were round holes in the plastic where you inserted your fingers to dial the numbers. Sometimes when Caroline was on the phone, she hooked her fingers into those holes.

The root of the word *dial* is *dies*, in Latin, *day*: *dialis* means daily. The medieval Latin is *rotus dialis*, the daily wheel, which evolved to mean any round dial over a plate. It is hard to convey now the heat of the old phone receiver, the curve of it on your mouth. If someone spoke into the receiver quietly, his lips would brush the tiny holes. There was the phone smell of plastic rimmed with overheated air. If you cut the cord, or the phone for some reason was yanked out of the wall, say, you saw that the wires inside the cord were brightly colored: blue, yellow, red, green. It was complicated, the business of talking. Caroline liked black phones. Usually, then, when the phone rang, it was Alastair, but to pick up the phone she had to be home.

The second way to make a call was to use a public telephone. There were phone booths on the corners of many streets. Always at the corner, never in the middle of the block. There were public telephones in drugstores and restaurants. You said to whoever was around, the girl behind the cash register, the man behind the counter: Can I use your phone? Or, if you wanted to use the telephone in the street and needed change, you asked if you could change a dollar for quarters, *for the phone*. The phone booths on the street were made of metal and heavy glass. Later in New York the phone booths became fewer in neighborhoods where drug dealers used them to schedule drops. Because of this you had to sometimes walk for blocks in the snow or the rain to find a phone.

It was warm in the phone booth and usually dry. Often people left things in phone booths: umbrellas, packages, wallets. They were distracted when talking on the phone, by what they were saying, or by what was being said to them. There was a bifold door to shut, for privacy. If you stayed too long in the phone booth, the windows fogged up; if you went inside after someone else had been inside a long time, it was foggy with their breath. The call was a dime, then it was fifteen cents, then a quarter. The public phones were rectangular, and there were three slots for coins on the phone, on the top; the slot for the dime was in the right upper corner. The receiver was connected to the phone by a cord. In the phone booth, the radius in which you could pace while you made a call was constricted; you shifted from foot to foot. In every case, no matter where you were calling from, there was a specified circumference, a radius, in which you could make a phone call, a certain distance and not more, from the place where the phone was connected to the earth, to the ganglion of wires that spanned out from the phone. Time was money. A long call cost more than a short one. When Caroline made a call from a telephone box, if it went on for more than three minutes the operator would come on the line and say, *Five cents more, please*. She scrounged for nickels, for dimes, later for quarters, in the pocket of her jacket, which had a hole. Coins slipped through and weighed down the lining as if she were planning to drown herself in the river.

When Caroline was a teenager, talking on the phone, it wasn't unusual for the operator to break into a call: "Your father wants to get through on this line." At the house where she went to the beach in the summer, there was a party line: five families on the road shared a number. If you picked up the phone and heard voices, the rule was: put it down. But everyone knew everyone's business. Now there are ways to accomplish the same thing—the sense of being known; the world is a party line. Then people called "collect" when they did not have money for the phone, when they either did not have it or could not find the change. You could call the operator without a coin, and she would put the call through. In a "collect" call someone at the other end of the line picked up the receiver, and the operator said, "Caroline is calling, will you accept the charges?" What if he said no? The shame of it. There was no way to leave a message; it wasn't until 1986 that Caroline had an answering machine, which plugged into the phone and flashed a tiny little red warning light—then as now, there could be messages you did not want to hear. Along any road in the country the telephone poles stretched for miles, timber poles with wires looping over them, a chain stitch across the map, birds weighing down the wires, storms knocking them over. There were men whose job it was to repair those wires, sitting up on the poles. In the catbird seat. Up the mast. Gone now, the ruled paper lines the wires made in the air, music paper unfolding through the forests, on which voices sang, argued, planned, began, and ended things. A call from far away was a "long-distance" call.

Because phones were rooted to the spot, if someone called you and you picked up, they knew where you were, and if you did not answer they knew you were not there, which sometimes meant that you were not where you said you were. In Manhattan, the phone numbers gave it away: CHelsea 3, MUrray Hill 7. Caroline's exchange was TRafalgar 7. You could not say you were one place and be in another; location services could not be *switched off*. Birds perched on the wires, black notes, arpeggios. Standing in the park by the ball fields, Caroline had her cell phone in her glove so that she would feel it on her palm if he called.

In the same few hundred square yards where Caroline is waiting for a phone call—at a time that has been prearranged, which turns out to be a time when Caroline, who has forgotten her morning schedule completely, had an appointment on the East Side and is now, instead, standing in the park, freezing, as she did not want to answer the telephone, if and when it rang, on the crosstown bus, windows steamy with condensation, or in a taxi—Alastair is crouched in the dark, forty years ago, writing his name in the frozen dirt by the ball fields with a stick. He is fifteen. He is wearing a down jacket which is too small for him and which has been handed down to his brother, but he does not want to give it up, because he likes the way it smells. The feathers are coming out, pricking the nylon with little quills. Underneath he has on his school button-down shirt. The shirt is white, and a little grubby. The tails are out. His sneakers are wet from the snow. At school, in French class, they had been shown a film, *L'enfant sauvage*. He is underdressed for the weather, but he is thinking about the naked wild child, Victor, in Aveyron. Did he never have

any clothes? How can that be? He imagines being naked in
the woods, the cold puckering his body. He has looked up
the weather in rural France. At night in the forest, it can dip
below freezing. Alastair imagines the boy digging a burrow in
the earth and covering himself with leaves. At the Museum of
Natural History, where he had been taken by his nanny two
or three times a week in the afternoons after school, there is a
room where you can see mice and shrews in their lairs under
the snow. There are little tunnels under the earth that end
in sometimes large, intricate rooms, filled with treasures and
food, old nuts, wizened berries. In one the mouse looks frightened, as if he (or she: was it a girl mouse or a boy mouse?) had
just fled from something menacing on the crust of the earth
over the burrow. That is what it looks like, in the cross section
of the glass: the crust of the earth. It is fraying a little, like an
old piece of toast, the hard dirt over the burrow, frosted with
snow. Alastair named the mouse Mike. "*Ssh,*" he said to Mike,
touching his nose through the tempered glass. "How ya doing,
Mike," his brother, Otto said, leering, making scary faces at the
mouse. But Mike, who was stuffed, did not move. There was
no taunting him. They did not know then that later, at least for
a little while, it would be Alastair who would save Otto. There
was no saving Alastair. In the park in the cold at eight in the
evening on a Wednesday night when he has told his mother he
is working on his project about batteries or tree sap with his
friend Jason on Central Park West, Alastair moves away from
the ball fields—he is now about one hundred yards from where
Caroline is standing—and into a grove of locust trees, which
later would shrivel. In a storm in 1996 they were toppled by the
wind and then cleared. Locusts have shallow roots. Under the
dirt the roots are in the way, the roots are everywhere. Alastair

has no tool but his pocketknife. He is thinking about Mike, and the wild boy, and the shape of the burrow he would make, like a canoe in the dirt. He wants to take off his clothes and cover himself with leaves. In the morning, he will wake up and everything will be quite different. The park will no longer be the park but another place in the woods. He will be on an island that has not been discovered by anyone, full of leafy trees and streams, and he will go down to the stream and drink water by cupping his hands. Little fish will swim through his fingers. His grandfather walked with him in the woods in the summer. If he was lost, he was to listen for the sound of water. If you were lost at sea and saw a bird, that meant you were near land. In the winter though, Alastair thought, the water is frozen and there is no sound. When he passed it earlier in the day the Boat Pond had a lid of ice. His pocketknife is ineffectual, and he nicks the blade on a locust root or a stone. He pictures the burrow in his mind and unbuttons his shirt, his hands moving onto his skin.

Caroline is standing in the snow. She is so cold that the phrase *freezing to death* enters her mind. She is wondering if she is standing in exactly the right place. She knows about the burrow, and Mike the mouse. She thinks about what she knows about telephones. When she dials a number, does it shoot up to a satellite and then back down? Ordinary telephone conversations have always been mysterious to her. By ordinary she still means the kind of phone call that is attached to a wall by a black snake of wire. She likes picturing the conversations shooting over the tendrils. In the film *Sunday Bloody Sunday*, a triangle of lovers leave messages for each other along those wires. The conversations are irradiated by color, red, yellow, green. For a long time, Caroline thought that she was the single woman in that film who pours yesterday's cold coffee into her cup, stubs out her cigarette on the carpet, and is thwarted and betrayed by the man with whom she is in love, a mophead—it's 1971—who makes light-filled glass sculptures and who also loves an older man who has a surgery in Harley Street. But she is wrong. In the film, the mophead betrays both of his lovers, but she has not been betrayed, because in her own life nothing has been kept from her: she simply wants something that is not there, which she has been told is not there, but she thinks if she keeps wanting it, her desire will be like water on a stone, things will change. A form of magical thinking, making something out of nothing. Caroline knows and does not know this. But she is in hiding under the mask of the woman who stubs out her cigarette, because she is also the man who makes glass sculptures which fill at dusk with blue light, a person who loves two or even three people at once. (Or, she used to be that person. Now she is not.) What she likes is theater, the glass tubes filling with light. Alastair knows this about her; he also knows that he can stop her heart, which he is doing right now, because he has not called and she is freezing to death, one hundred paces from where there was once a grove of locust trees, where in another diamond of time, he is trying to cut a root with his penknife, a present from his uncle Link on his tenth birthday. Snow is falling down around both of them. A jangle of bells. There is nothing more beautiful, said Frank O'Hara, in a poem whose name she cannot now remember, a poem with long lines, like telephone wires, than the lights turning from red to green on Park Avenue during a snowstorm. Park Avenue is about a ten-minute walk from where she is standing, with her phone in her glove, if she could move. But she is like a figure in a snow globe.

(Now you ask, the first sign of you, to whom I am telling this story: Then, she also liked to talk on the phone? When I was a child, we used a *gettone*: *"Non sei mai solo quando sei vicino a un telefono!"* That was the slogan. "You're never alone when you're near a telephone." Maybe yes, maybe no.)

*

In the story of the Snow Queen, two children love each other. Every time she reads it, it stops Caroline's heart. The children are Gerda and Kai. The story is really about Gerda and Kai, but nevertheless it is the Snow Queen's story, a cold stone at the heart of love, skidding across an icy pond. The children live quite close to each other in a town—they can climb into each other's houses by jumping from terrace to terrace. Her father, too, went from terrace to terrace in Brooklyn, when he was a boy. He leapt, his foot in his leather shoe grazing the porch railing. Gerda lives with her grandmother. In the spring and long into the autumn there is a beautiful trellis of red roses on their terrace. Gerda and Kai both look forward every year to the time when the roses begin to bloom. The story divides in three parts. *You take this one*, says the fairy. That is the trouble with choices: they are one thing, or another. In the first part of the story, the devil himself makes a magic mirror that reflects everything beautiful in the world back as something drab and terrible; the translation from the Danish is peculiar: *wet spinach*. Can that be right? The devil is so proud of his mirror, he takes it up to heaven for the angels to admire, but on the way down, he drops it and the mirror shatters into a million pieces and falls to earth. Some of the shards are no bigger than a piece of grit. They float around still today, and get in your eye unexpectedly and make you cry. One day as Gerda and Kai are playing, it is autumn and the last roses are the most beautiful, cupping the faint sun in their petals, Kai gets a splinter in his eye. At first it simply blinds him. He asks Gerda to bathe it, and she runs inside for a cool cloth. But when his eye stops smarting, the sun has gone behind the clouds. Now, to Kai, the roses look like old shoe leather and Gerda is too stupid, with her damp cloth and her worried look. It begins to snow, large soft flakes as big as pinwheels. The snow piles up in the plaza. Kai takes his sled, which has silver runners. Gerda runs to put on her boots. He berates her for being so slow, and he jumps on the sled and leaves her behind. The snow is coming down unnaturally fast. There is a faint jangle of bells, and a sleigh appears, and the bells call to him, *Come away. Come away,* the bells said to Kai, when he looked up from his sled in the town square.

The sleigh is silver, and the woman driving it is barely visible in the gale, because she is wearing clothes which are made of cold moonlight. She is mad. Her bridle is made of pewter. Her white hair, streaming behind her, would reach the ground if she stood. *Come,* she says to Kai. Her voice is the only thing he can hear. It is not above the wind but inside it. It is made of spun sugar, that voice. His eyes hurt, and he tries to rub the grit out of them with his mitten, which is stiff with ice. The crystals rake his face, and he cuts himself above his left eye. The rose-red blood splotches the snow where, later, Gerda will find it. The voice speaking is the voice of the Snow Queen. *Now,* she says. Kai's body strains toward the voice and as it does, ice enters him through the cut over his brow and he can no longer hold his sled with his frozen fingers. He has become a frozen silk thread pulled through the eye of a needle. The sled careens away from him and smashes at the foot of the elm tree in the center of the square, on the octagonal bench where in fine weather the old people sit and fan themselves. One of the runners is bent and a strut is smashed. Later, Gerda will take it to her uncle, the blacksmith, to see if he can mend it for Kai when he returns. But Kai is gone. When his sled fell from him, he gripped the lariat of bells on the Snow Queen's sleigh, which are so cold they burn, and in an instant, he is on the sleigh, and the barbed wire lariat is tied tight around him, to no purpose because he is transfixed, it would not occur to him to get away. But later he will have welts on his back that will never disappear entirely, not even when he is an old man, living in the woods, writing, blind in one eye. But that is much later, we will not get to the end of the story for a little while. *If thy right eye offend thee.*

*

Caroline is a few yards from the now-gone theater of locust trees, where Alastair broke his knife—a nebula of star matter, a mouse in a burrow, a boy covered with leaves who loses the ability to speak, a conversation that hummed along loping wires, a few blocks from the museum, where under a high windowed ceiling, in a room named for a boy who disappeared in an upturned canoe, there is a row of nutmeg tree trunks, standing on end, their roots whittled to look like wings. The wild boy of Aveyron was born in 1788. There were sightings of a boy as early as 1794. A green boy, rather than a green man. A boy who had scars on his body, who was mute, who might or might not have been abused, who had no language. Would he have grown up to be a Green Man? In church architecture, there are three versions of the Green Man: the foliate head, completely covered in leaves; the disgorging head, spewing vegetation from the mouth; and the bloodsucker head, leaves sprouting from every orifice. Jean Marc Gaspard Itard, the medical student who cared for Victor, the wild boy, believed there were two things that separated humans from animals: the capacity for empathy and the ability to speak.

⊥

It is winter and there are no leaves on the locust trees. In the dark Alastair has given up hacking at the roots with his penknife to make himself a burrow. He puts his clothes back on. He is skating, he knows, on how late he can be, before there is a chance—a chance—that his mother will look up Jason's number and call to find him, and then find out that Alastair has not been there, that Jason's mother knows nothing about a battery project. There is little chance of this. Alastair is at Jason's because Jason's mother is not home, she goes out every night, and he knows that if Jason picks up the phone—if Jason is there, and not at his girlfriend Willa's on Seventy-Second Street, whose parents are in London and whose housekeeper is dozing in front of the television in the maid's room—he will automatically lie to Alastair's mother, and say that Alastair has *just left*. He will lie without thought, like Pavlov, when he hears Alastair's mother's voice, which he knows, as he and Alastair have been friends since nursery school, he will automatically say that Alastair is not here, or wherever, or whatever he should be doing; Jason will represent Alastair as whatever he knows Alastair's mother wants him to be: a boy who has just eaten macaroni and cheese for supper, made by Viola, the housekeeper,

and finished his notes for the day on the battery project, tucked
in his shirt, and zipped up his jacket before calling for the elevator man to take him down eleven stories so he could walk
the few blocks home.

None of this will happen. Alastair's mother is watching a
production of *Moonchildren* at the Royale Theatre on Forty-Fifth
Street. Then she will go to Elaine's. She is wearing a peacock-
blue shift with gold buttons and high-heeled black pumps by
Delman, which she regrets wearing, because, of course, it is
snowing. She is wearing a black wool trench coat, to the knee,
and a hat that is very similar to the one that Caroline is wearing, forty years later, in the snow, a fox hat, while she waits
for the phone to buzz under her glove. When Caroline and
Alastair were small children, on different "game tables," or on
the floor in different cottages made of planked pine in the summer, they played board games. Parcheesi—the rules of which
Caroline could never remember—Clue, Monopoly. The game
she is thinking of now is Operation: the board was not exactly
a board, but a pictograph of a human body, called Cavity Sam,
with a red nose that lit up. At the beginning of each round,
each player was dealt a "doctor card." The goal was to remove
the offending ailment from Cavity Sam, with a pair of twee-
zers, without knocking into Sam's body. It was hard to do. The
plastic parts fit snugly into the shapes carved out on his torso
and arms and legs. If you were clumsy, Sam's lightbulb nose lit
up: *out.* The list of ailments included Wish Bone, Butterflies in
Stomach, Writer's Cramp, and Broken Heart. When a few days
ago she had looked up the rules of this game, she found that
by lingering on the word *wish* it appeared in yellow, as if in a
smudge of butter. With a click, *wish* leads her to a song called

"I Wish You Could Have Turned My Head (And Left My Heart Alone)" by Sonny Throckmorton, which in turn leads her to *mercury*, which can refer to an element, a planet, a Roman god, a rock star, and many other things. There is no end to it, she thinks.

When Caroline was eight, she was a Brownie for about five minutes. She wore a brown uniform which had a space above the left breast pocket for medals. She did not have breasts, and she did not stay long enough to win any medals. From those two weeks, she remembers only a tiny song and a rhyme, and a piece of aluminum foil that the troop leader had cut into a large circle and placed on the floor. The troop leader was her best friend's mother, the only grown-up Caroline called by her first name, although she knew without being told that this was not allowed at Brownies. When Caroline took time to think about these weeks, she realized the circle of foil must have been a number of pieces of tinfoil, taped together; one thing Caroline knows about now is tinfoil. The Brownies met in the gym of the elementary school, or at least that is what Caroline recalls. Her memory can be faulty. As she remembers it, the tiny song went like this:

> *What have I in my shirt pocket, in a handy place?*
> *I keep it very close to me, it can never be replaced*
> *Even if you asked me thrice I know I wouldn't tell*
> *My Brownie Smile is mine for keeps—I asked the Wishing Well.*

Her memory is faulty. She did not remember the name of this song, only the hum of it in the back of her brain, a place she avoids, a small room where certain buzzings are stored, hummings that sound like the beginning of wind from far off, a low hiss whose effect is to make her heart beat faster. When she was a child, her father sang her folk songs and nursery rhymes—*In Dublin's fair city, where the girls are so pretty*. But when she found the song, her fingers clicking through the possible permutations: for who knew—sitting in the typing class where the desks were bolted to the seats, at the same desk she had dived under during an air raid drill, told to cover her head with her hands, over or under the braids, as her braids began, always, high up, over her ears—that everyone would become a typist, that it would no longer be a skill to "fall back on" if other ideas failed, that the keyboard on which her fingers walked into the labyrinth of herself would become for everybody, everywhere, a sort of acid trip to worlds circling worlds, the information carefully doled out so that unless you were skillful you were consistently led away from the main point? When she found the list of Girl Scout songs, split into categories, one of which was "Generic Graces"—an idea she found momentarily so enchanting and depressing that she had to pull herself away from it by force, as if bending a spoon—she knew it immediately: the "Brownie Smile Song."

The song pitched Caroline back. Her mother had recently had her hair cut almost to her shoulders. Her braids stuck out. Her face was round. A mole on her leg was too high up to scratch. Caroline was a girl whose face was naturally solemn, to whom strangers in the street, even when she was small and walking with her mother, and later, certainly, when she was on her own, on the way to meet a friend or heading into the subway, said, "Smile!" or "Come on, a pretty girl like you, things can't be so bad," a girl at whom older women gazed, on buses and in coffee shops, with looks of compassionate inquiry (now

that Caroline is older, she gives similar girls this look, and they
burst into tears: she is under the impression that this is compassionate, which may or may not be so). The brute fact is that
she has a transforming smile. She knows this because she has
been told it over and over. It's as if people know this, and when
they ask her to smile, they want something of her—it still happens, and often she resents it. Do they want her to be transformed, or do they want to be transformed by her smile—or
do they want for reasons of their own for Caroline to be happy,
because it means she's happy with them, which is another thing
they want, and want the smile as evidence? All of which makes
smiling, still, difficult for Caroline. Oh stop, I can hear you
saying as you listen, idly, to this musing aloud, the second notice of you in this story, an appearance which is here simply a
conduit for you to gesticulate, to say, Don't be an imbecile, to
say, Caroline likes talking so much that she complicates things
for herself and everyone else, while you prefer silence—*stare
zitto*. (Another link which also enchants Caroline, but which
she has not tried, because she's afraid she would never emerge,
is Babylon Translator.) Recently she reread a story in which an
unlikable character called Ninetta doles out her smile "like a
precious jewel" and thought, not favorably, of herself. Recently,
she has been doing this quite a bit, smiling, wrapped in a white
terry-cloth bathrobe, the kind that is available for a price from
hotels, sitting cross-legged in a tangle of sheets, drinking a tiny
cup of coffee.

But at eight years old, Caroline was less—malleable. She
did not give herself away easily. She didn't know yet that it was
impossible, it would never be possible, for her to give herself
away, no matter how hard she tried: she was stuck with herself,

and the smile song was about as close to an assault as she could imagine, then. She did not have a smile in her pocket; she did not want to put a smile on her face. None of that was exactly true. She did have a smile in her pocket, but it was not a real smile; it was a pretend smile. Now, that dichotomy is not one she would be so quick to recognize. It is a kind of splitting of hairs she has given up on. But at eight she had a need to orient herself, which is an attribute of Girl Guides and generals, and can lead to draconian measures. This isn't entirely absent from Caroline's makeup now, to perhaps the same unfortunate effect—that is, she has been wondering, lately, whether she is a fanatic. The smile song, that first week, was Caroline's first inkling, the first dull roots of disappointment, that she would not stay a Brownie, and one day graduate, her chest full of medals, and become a Girl Scout. The smile song was Caroline's cherry tree: she could not tell a lie. She did not have her smile in her pocket. Her concept of literature and history was deep but hazy, a vivid dream, a befuddlement that would remain, long past the time when clarity might have been expected; the cherry tree George Washington cut down was also the tree where Abraham raised the knife over Isaac and was stilled by the voice of God; it was the cherry tree which is cut down in the last scene of *The Cherry Orchard*, a thwack that many years later made her eldest daughter cry out "No!" in a movie theater on East Sixty-Eighth Street, where she had taken her girls to see a film of the play starring Charlotte Rampling as Madame Ranevskaya, and Alan Bates as Gayev. *Non piangere sul latte versato?* you ask me. Yes.

The rhyme was at the center of a story. There was a little girl named Mary, who lived with her grandmother. In many of the stories that were read to Caroline, and then those she read to herself and later read to her own children, a mother has been made to disappear, as if a maternal presence in itself kept stories from unfolding. These were stories in which she felt at home, but until many years later, when a friend said it was almost impossible to find stories with mothers—her own daughter did not want to read stories in which the mother was dead or absent—she hadn't noticed this, as she herself had no mother to speak of, and until very recently had never identified with the mother in a story, only with the child, as if becoming a mother herself was almost accidental, like turning into a tree or a bird in a fairy tale. Her own children did not seem to mind stories in which the mother died, or disappeared on a long trip, never to return, or only to return after the adventure was tidied away, leaving with only a sharp glance meaning *hush!* across the table. In the Brownie story, there is no explanation why Mary goes to live with her grandmother—she just does. She has a brother, called Tommy, but he is not essential, indeed, in the poem he's entirely forgotten. The phrase she used this morning to dismiss her youngest daughter, who had gotten up and was rubbing her eyes on the veranda, to look out at the palm trees (she had taken them, as she had been taken as a child, for a week by the sea in the middle of winter), was "I am working for half an hour and then I will be entirely yours." Her children are the only people to whom Caroline has ever belonged entirely. Her own mother, if not wholly absent, was misplaced; in any case, she had never belonged to Caroline, even for a minute. In the story, Mary and Tommy are slovenly and ill-mannered. Their grandmother tells them about the Brownies, tiny people who are good and kind and helpful but who have left in despair, because they are too small to clean up the mess made by Mary and Tommy. Mary wants to see the Brownies, she wants to *be* a Brownie; she is a spoiled child, she stamps her foot. Her grandmother is firm: if Mary wants to see the Brownies, she must find the old owl who lives in the forest.

She listens for the owl hooting and follows the sound. The woods are dark and deep. When she finds him—the owl is an old grandfather, a troubadour of the woods, Churchill in a pith helmet—he gives her instructions. He laughs at her: it is a horrible sound, the owl laughing in dark trees. She must go down to the pond at the end of the lane when the moon is full. What she must do then, the owl says, is turn herself around three times, while saying verses for which he gives her the first line, but she must make the second line rhyme. Mary goes down the dark lane to the pond where muck grips her ankles. Frogs are calling in the wet dark. Moonlight skims the shiny water. What does she chant? Words Caroline learned, later.

> *Twist me and turn me and show me the elf*
> *I looked in the mirror and saw—*

It is too hard to find the missing word. She returns to the sinister owl, the death mask in the trees, for now he is all sound, hoot, and cackle, and he says, "Go back."

When Caroline was a child she watched television with her mother. There was one game show she liked in particular: the announcer canvassed the audience for loot. (Was he an MC, an announcer, the host? Over time she has lost the lingo of TV, its peculiar patois.) Does anyone have a boiled egg, a quill pen, a kitten? People brought huge carryall bags. A compass, a bullhorn, a fishing rod, a map of Saskatchewan? It was the reverse of the peddler's cry: caps for sale, knives sharpened, the ragman, the iceman cometh. When Caroline was small the milkman delivered bottles to the back door, and the metal lid on the box clanged when he left. Her mother kept even the screen door locked. Mary Poppins had a carpetbag from which she unpacked a standing lamp, a parrot umbrella, her best hat. An assortment of objects could turn into magic. If you had an egg, a pen, and a kitten, you earned three wishes: door number one, door number two, and door number three. If you chose the right door, you won: a car, a deluxe vacuum cleaner, cash. Caroline had no use for any of these things. She liked it best when the contestant chose the wrong door: a cartful of pigs, a thousand plastic whistles. Later, when she fell in love with Joseph Cornell, she thought of those whistles. He lived alone with his brother and his mother on Utopia Parkway, and she thought, too, of Pavese, whom she also loved.

> *Ancora cadrà la pioggia*
> *sui tuoi dolci selciati*

Like Morandi, who painted cityscapes of bottles.

There were only three doors, and three wishes. It was a rule she understood, then. But if one did not have an egg or a pen, or a bottle of Coke, it was impossible even to wish. It was necessary to be prepared, to think ahead about what might be wanted, to have at the ready what you might be asked to give. By preparing and supplying what was wanted to create a need for that very thing. Very recently, Caroline wrote in a letter—or what today passes for a letter—*I wish—but* . . . Wishing is when she is least imaginative. It amounts to whistling in the dark.

When Mary returned to the owl, he sent her back to the dark road and the black pond. What was so terrifying about the task, to Caroline? Caroline at eight, the waist of the Brownie skirt pinching above the elastic of her knickers, which left a red band on her waist that circled her like a garrote, when she took her bath? At the Brownie meeting, she is gazing at the pond made of tinfoil on the floor of the gymnasium. The floor smells of wax. The troop leader, who is the mother of her friend, who cannot be called by her name but has turned into ma'am—yes ma'am, no ma'am—has cut some branches and arranged them prettily around the tinfoil pond. They are rowan branches, from the hedge outside the school, with pinkish rather than white blossoms. When P. L. Travers came to visit Yeats, she arrived with an armful of rowan branches, and he remarked that one would have been enough.

It is bad luck to bring rowan branches into a house—how does Caroline know that? Perhaps she knew it only later, per- haps she learned it from Yeats—but perhaps the school gym- nasium does not count. "Turn yourself around three times." For Caroline now, even the idea of rhyme is exhausting. The idea of making something *come out*. Come out of the shadow of this red rock. A few weeks ago a boy said to her—a boy who is in some ways in her care, although entrusting anything to Caroline is foolish—a boy who each week has a new drawing of a bird tattooed on his scalp, a bird from a book of fifteen Japanese drawings from the fifteenth century, a boy who has no hair because chemicals have burned it away, a boy who has had so much radiation that he cannot have any more because he would become a *public health hazard*, said to her: "Rhyme is always an act of desperation." Of course, he did not know he was talking to Caroline. When he speaks to her he has another person in mind, or at least she thinks he does. He does her the courtesy of pretending. In a different life, she would be in love with this boy. She knows it and he knows it. Perhaps he is entrusted, really, to that person, who is not Caroline. Rhyme is only language playing catch with itself, isn't that so? So why was it so terrifying?

She stood in line in the gym. She was third, there were seven little girls in Brownie uniforms. Two girls ahead of her, four girls behind her. Her friend's long blond braid smelled of sulphur; she used a special shampoo on her hair, Caroline knew. There was another odor, which later she would be able to identify as rowan. She was in Sussex, visiting a friend, and when she broke off a branch her friend, a woman with wild hair and blue eyes, whose father had been poet laureate of England, a woman who looked like Maud Gonne, said, "Don't bring it in the house." The friend had a hedge made of elderberry. She watched the first girl, turned around by her friend's mother, a woman who had become a stranger, say the rhyme. She did not see her friend turn around, because by then her eyes were closed. She was still close to the age when it is possible to think that if you close your eyes you disappear. Her brother was two, and he believed it. He would grow up into a man who thought he could make other people disappear, whether his eyes were open or shut, but she remembered it, and when she closed her eyes she wished she still believed it instead of half believing it.

She didn't disappear. Through what she would later know
was proprioception, she could feel her fingers and her feet in
their lace-up shoes on the waxed floor, and the hand on her
shoulder. She could hear her name. She was a child who was
eager to please, or if not eager to please eager to avoid giving
displeasure—although she learned too early that not pleas-
ing was a form of power, but she knew with the same leaden
feeling that prevented her later from just going along with it,
whatever it was, even if it seemed she was going along with
it at the time, and helping or even taking charge of it, that she
was not in the end, whenever that came, going to be able to go
through with it. She could not open her eyes and be turned
around three times. She could not say the rhyme which would
turn her from an imp into a Brownie. She would not look into
the tinfoil pond wreathed with the lethal rowan branches that
brought the smell of death into the waxy linseed smell of the
gymnasium, and say that when she looked into the tin pond
(Caroline knew about tin; she had been taken as a small child
to a tin mine in Jamaica by her father, and seen the red rock,
and stood in the shadow of an enormous machine that pulled
the tin out of the rock, she was told, like a magnet, and had
been given lemonade to drink under a green-and-white-striped
awning) she saw—herself. If you had asked her at that moment
why, she would not have answered, or been able to answer. In
those days children had their mouths washed out with soap.
Not something you hear of now. It had not happened to her but
she knew it could. If she had been screwed to the wall or made
to confess by having stones loaded on her in a narrow grave,
she would have said she thought it was silly, it was ridiculous
to be asked to say a rhyme and look into a pond made of tinfoil

and expect something to happen. None of the words that she uses easily now, that everyone now uses easily, would have entered or left her mouth.

Twist me and turn me and show me the elf
I looked in the mirror and saw—

The dictionary doesn't link *terror*, which comes from the French *terroir*, which means "great fear, dread," from the root *tre*, to shake, or tremble, and *terra*—earth—dry land, as in *terra firma*, but imbedded in *terra firma* is the idea that the earth could shake. Anything can happen. One thing can become another. All children know this. Eyes closed, in the crocodile of girls dressed up as Brownies, Caroline was meant to turn, or be turned by the hand on her shoulder, three times, and when she looked into the tinfoil, which was at first a pond and was now a mirror, she would see herself transformed into a Brownie, a creature of the woods who was helpful, kind, and good. It would only work if she said the rhyme. The rhyme was a charm. When she shut her eyes and refused to be budged by the hand on her shoulder, a hand both known and unknown (Had that hand touched her before? Probably, but not certainly), it was because she knew that for her to turn three times was to risk vanishing. Later she would describe moments in which events drifted toward inescapable disaster as "watching a car wreck," or "falling out of an airplane"—the moment when the uncanny trembles just out of sight, the place from which it is impossible to exit, the bolt shot. One is always a paying guest; sooner or later, the tab comes due; George Emerson says to Lucy Honeychurch as they gaze into the Arno, "'I did mind them so, and one is so foolish, it seemed better that they should go out to the sea—I don't know; I may just mean that they frightened me.' Then the boy verged into a man. 'For something tremendous has happened; I must face it without getting muddled. It isn't exactly that a man has died.' Something warned Lucy that she must stop him. 'It has happened,' he repeated, 'and I mean to find out what it is.'" Much later Caroline would have a daughter with blue eyes set far apart, who, watching a film made from this, at thirteen, would remark, "Why *say* that it has happened at all? That is his mistake."

*

Each snarled thread leads to something else, many other things, too many: wishes, charms, Caroline at eight in a too-snug Brownie uniform, looking at a mirror wreathed in dangerous rowan leaves, a mirror that might as well be a sheet of ice. A sheet of ice she is trying to clear with a gloved hand, in order to see Alastair, who has given up chopping at the root of the locust tree with his penknife. Five or six years after Caroline stood in the snow waiting for Alastair to call, her cell phone in her fur-lined glove, she is lying full-length on her bed in New York, dressed for a party, although she has kicked off her shoes. The party is over. It is eleven o'clock at night and her son, George, who is twenty-one and is wearing a long bead necklace, a white shirt, and blue jeans, is lying beside her. They are eating leftover chocolate almonds, and George is drinking something pink—the remains of the vodka punch. He is asking Caroline what *insular* means. She immediately thinks of his packed lunches, with the little thermos full of cocoa. Narrow-minded, she says.

It was his birthday party. At supper, when he sat down beside her at the table for a minute, he told her that there are people who have small magnets embedded in their fingertips so that they can sense force fields—electric plants, storms. "It is like having another sense," he said. "We used to be sensitive to auras and now we are not." Caroline was alarmed by this. The idea of choosing to be more aware made her head spin. Her skin prickles when there is an electric storm forty miles away. George was annoyed. Sometimes, he told her, the force is so great that the magnets turn over under their skin. Caroline excused herself from the table. When the children were small the number of candles was important, one for each year and one for good luck, all blown out by a single breath and a wish you could not tell or it would not come true. *Come truly to me, under the windblown leaves, and I will make a fiddle of your breast bone.* But there are so many birthday candles now, she doesn't bother to count them but sticks them willy-nilly into the cake.

The other night, do you remember, we walked down to the river through the park, the sky was lavender and pink, past the boat basin, where Alastair and Caroline used to watch the trash wash up and scuttle and congregate along the bank, the houseboats alight then, like hives over the water—an impossible and incongruent image: honey and salt. You said you had always wanted to live on the river, in a houseboat. But now it is years ago, and now two miles away, on the northwest axis, Caroline is standing with her feet in ice, in the northeast quadrant of Central Park. Chutes and Ladders. There is another game she liked, but it came later; a set of cards in a little box called Oblique Strategies. She had first seen the cards dealt by a young woman trapeze artist, who wore little black pointed boots that

matched her raven cap of hair. Her name was Maudie. She liked
to rig herself up in winter on a swing over waterfalls, wearing
petticoats with long underwear underneath, and swing so she
looked like spray from the falls. The performances were charming and mad. In New Hampshire, the police came and put a stop
to them. She was both a private and a public nuisance. They met
at an artists' retreat, where Caroline was supposed to be writing
a book in her solitary icy cabin, but was instead talking on the
telephone and driving to Maine to see Alastair, down hairpin
turns skiddy with ice, in the middle of the night, to a ramshackle
house by a cove where he was camped, that winter, on a mat-
tress, to which he had brought a cookbook called *Gluten-Free
Suppers*, because he was under the impression, which Caroline
did not out of pity tell him was false, that his daughters, who
could not digest wheat, would come to visit him and he would
cook them supper. He had also brought his dog. The first time
Caroline and the dog met, he would not leave her side. When
she went to the bathroom in the dark, navigating the steep stairs
she had known as a girl, he came with her, and put his head
on her knee, as if he had found, finally, an ally, someone who
might come to his aid. *Help at last*, his gaze said. He was a large,
graying black Labrador, a dog who looked as if at any moment
he might recite Edmund's speech, "The wheel is come full circle,
I am here." His muzzle was velvet on her thigh, and damp. The
sound of the tide, in and out, was steady and loud, a kind of
radio static in which if she could just change the frequency she
would understand—what? The dog speaking to her? What kind
of animal are you, if you could come back as an animal? A game
she had played with her cousins, in an apartment on Park Avenue where green leatherette peeled off the walls of the elevator.

The cards came—the first set, at least—in a dark blue shagreen box. They were a collaboration between the musician Brian Eno and the writer Peter Schmidt. Each card was printed, like the strip of paper inside a fortune cookie, with an adage meant to illuminate a juncture—a decision point—in life or work. For example, a card picked from the deck—because it is a pack of cards, it carries with it all the melodies of chance, *of winning and losing*, about which Caroline was like the boy with his finger in the dike, so set against the flood, for no reason at all except that *she did not go along with things*—reads: "What wouldn't you do?" What wouldn't Caroline do? Not to her credit, she thinks, the list is short. It seems to her that there may be no end to the possibilities for bad behavior, for opportunities in which to be abject—and even fewer in which a kind of loyalty—think of Gerda, listening for the bells, her ear to the ground—can be seen as sublime. A kind of excess clarity, she thinks. When George III visited Venice, he was honored at a banquet at which the white tablecloths, the serving dishes, the cutlery, were made of spun sugar. He never recovered—the snowy linen, the spoons, even the ice sculpture shaped like a swan, were made of fine sugar soft to the touch, like the sugar-coated Turkish delight by which Kai is lured into a sled by the jangling of bells. *Don't eat that*: the apple, the pomegranate seed. In yet another story, Harriet Vane is on trial for her life—she later marries the detective who has been obsessed *with proving her innocence*, a trope Caroline also likes—for killing a man with Turkish delight laced with arsenic. A cloud of sugar. Another card, one pulled from the deck this morning, reads, "Go outside. Shut the door." Outside of what? Caroline wonders.

She is so far inside herself that it is . . . implausible that she could or would "go outside." When Caroline and Alastair lived together, twenty-five years ago, they played at magic: the I Ching, the Tarot pack, the Ouija board. They were children. They liked games. She especially liked the feel of the planchette moving under her hands, as if a mouse had hoisted it on his shoulders, a little Atlas. Later the computer's mouse felt to her like the Ouija planchette, moving about the alphabet, talking nonsense, nonsense being desire expressed as fact: wishes made real. Caroline liked Oblique Strategies, because it was the kind of thing she liked—a nudge that opened a door— but also because when they were children, Alastair had played Brian Eno's *Another Green World* so constantly on the tape deck that the sound of it ground itself into her bones. The skittering opening bars, like squirrels, "I'll come running to tie your shoe." She pictured herself running to tie Alastair's shoes. When her children were small, the phrase often came to her mind, but she did not need to run, the children were always there, clinging to her leg. Perhaps that is why the dog, when she appeared, looked at her with such love, his nose wedging itself between her legs as she sat on the toilet listening to the sound of the waves, Alastair asleep upstairs, knotted in the sheets. The dog could not tie Alastair's shoes.

*

Caroline, standing in the middle of Central Park in a snowstorm, for it really is snowing now, as she waits for Alastair to call, begins to shift from foot to foot to keep warm. What she liked best about the Ouija board was the feeling of moving through the alphabet in space, a kind of phantom tollbooth, in which each letter was a door, a series of chutes or shunts which could become *yes*, or *yak*, or the beginning of *yes*, the *y* and then the *e* could become something else, a compromise or qualifier: *yet*. And yet. Not free. Farewell to an idea.

> *He says no to no and yes to yes. He says yes*
> *To no; and in saying yes he says farewell.*

Standing in the snow Caroline is on the verge of tears. There seems to be no line from *a* to *b*, or from *no* to *yes*. The language is lost in which she could speak to Alastair. Her old friend Maurice, now dead, death being what he most feared, the fear of nonbeing—what did he say? Her mind is blank, clawing at something in the cold. Oh yes, *If I had a mother who loved me* . . . Maurice's mother tried to end what would be Maurice—by jumping off the kitchen table. Maurice: *It was the dining room*. You didn't have a dining room, you lived in a tenement in Brooklyn with five people sleeping in one room. We had a dining room! Fine, the dining room, where you ate each other alive. So? Caroline's grandmother, too. An entire history of Russian Jewish women in New York, jumping off kitchen tables, the first story someone is told about themselves. Because she had not been wanted, her mother did not want Caroline. Fair is fair. In the snow, Caroline shifts from foot to foot. She is waiting for Alastair to call, twenty yards from where forty years ago he tried to cut a hole in the frozen ground in which to sleep, and when he could not do it, he nicked his arms with the penknife, a little trail of crosshatchings. Recently, a few years after Caroline stood in the snow, she went to a production of *Macbeth*, in a theater by the water, in Brooklyn. One actor played all the parts. The stage was set up as a hospital room, with an observation deck, so that from the stalls the room looked like an aquarium. The actor, his face like a cod, whose performance was a long scream, undulating at high frequencies, washed his red hands in the bathtub. Caroline had no idea he was a television star, the actor. The theater was packed, the audience laughing at the antics of a madman. When they left, the river was hurling itself against the breakwater.

*

When Caroline was a child, the one candy her mother liked was one that she did not. Licorice made her faintly sick, like the smell of gasoline. Later she would have a child who loved the smell of garages, the reek of oil and damp concrete. When this child was little, she loved the story of a crocodile mama who so likes perfume that she steals bottles from the department store perfume counter! Was Caroline a crocodile mother? She has no idea. The prey she swallows in one gulp is herself. When she sat on the sofa underneath the unfolded Chinese painting of a long black wave with black spittle, the man who emptied her pocket full of nightmares said, "What I am interested in is the story behind the story, under the black wave." The man said, "What constricts the heart is emotion that is withheld. What is that story? What emotion is it?" And she said, "Grief." She is like a pickup band learning tunes as she goes along and taking requests from the audience: "*Euch Lüften, die mein Klagen,*" "Swanee River," "Little Brown Jug," "Let's Call the Whole Thing Off." *But oh, if we call the whole thing off / . . . Then that might break*

my heart. Enough of that. *And when I die don't bury me at all, /
Just pickle my bones in alcohol.*

The truth changes as she gets hold of it, like a kite or a
snake; it does not like to be held, it thrashes.

In the snow in the park Caroline is listening for the sound
of bells, the bell that translates, in the century in which she
finds herself, to a telephone that vibrates in her hand, a tiny
electric shock. *I listen for the buzz of the telephone*—a song lyric
written by her daughter that she sings to her one hot night as
they cross Houston Street. That evening he spent freezing in the
park in his thin jacket, Alastair's mother did think of checking
to see if he was asleep when she got back from the theater—she
liked her children best when they were asleep, she sometimes
thought. In any case she forgot about it. If asked, she would
have said that she trusted all her children completely as they
had been brought up to tell the truth.

*

That morning in the swirling snow with the grit of the devil's
mirror in his eye, Kai disappears on the sleigh of the Snow
Queen. The Snow Queen has supped with the underworld,
a picnic by a pond that looked like a mirror, surrounded by
rowan. *Here*, said the underworld, *see how pretty you look*. Her
legs are open and he is speaking between them. The mirror is
above and below her but the Snow Queen's eyes are shut. Her
electric body is turning to dry ice. *Look in the mirror and you
will see*— Perhaps it is the space between the syllables that is
so frightening.

On the white sand
Of the beach of a small isle
In the Eastern Sea
I, my face streaked with tears,
Am playing with a crab
—ISHIKAWA TAKUBOKU

When Kai did not come back as he usually did in the late afternoon, to have tea with Gerda and her grandmother, whom she has been helping all afternoon—Christmas is coming, they are making cookies in the shapes of stars and trees—she went to the square and saw the splotch of blood, and under the tree, the sled in pieces. At first there is a search party, grown men in heavy jackets stomping through the snow, and women knocking on the doors of the houses that surround the plaza, asking whether someone has taken in an injured boy, who is even now resting on the sofa, his head bandaged. But they know he is gone. All the neighbors know Kai, and Gerda, and everyone else, too, and if Kai was hurt, someone would have sent for his mother. That his mother and father are away on a long trip to who knows where is no matter; they would have sent for Gerda, or her grandmother, or the housekeeper who has brought Kai up because they are so often not there, taking his sister with them, and leaving him with a round-faced woman who has an old ailing poodle and a carnelian ring. But they find nothing. Gerda knows they will not find him. She grows pale and thin, her gold hair dulling, but her eyes stay bright. She goes to school and helps her grandmother, but like all girls who are born looking for something they have lost, she is a fanatic. She loves Kai and refuses to believe he is lost to her. What she knows is that he has been taken from her and she must get him back. When she begins on her long journey to find him, taking her apron from around her waist and handing it to her grandmother—for she has bided her time and she is now too old for her grandmother to forbid her to go—she knows only that she must put one foot in front of the other. The only pull at her heart is that her grandmother is now so old. She takes her coat and an apple and her latchkey, so she can let herself in when she returns.

It is spring and the snow has melted. The angels who refused to look in the mirror—whom she encounters on her journey as birds and trees and the sun reflected in the puddles, and the moon, too, for she walks at night—talk among themselves but cannot help her. It is her own pure heart that will lead her to Kai. Anything they might add to her pocket to help would distract and hinder her. There is no riddle to ask a cat, no lucky card, no jacket to sew for a field mouse. Gerda knows, too, that she must not wish. She cannot wish for Kai to appear before her, because the only way to find him is to go to him. Nothing must deter her from putting one foot in front of the other. She must not wish for haste.

*

A number of years later, decades after Caroline had lived with Alastair and she was elsewhere in her life, she went to the movies almost every day. It did not matter particularly what movie, although she was under the impression that she chose them with some care. The film Caroline is watching—*The Company You Keep*—is not a very good film. She likes it for her own purposes. Nick and Mimi have not seen each other for twenty

years. It is unclear exactly what years we are talking about: the
actors are too old to have been student radicals in the sixties,
but let that be. A fictional story, based on facts. In the movie
there was actual footage: the March on Washington, the ruined
house on West Eleventh Street, ignited by the bomb factory in
the basement. The faces of the actors when they were young
had been superimposed on the clips, although at the time Robert Redford, who plays Nick in the movie, wasn't there; he was
in Hollywood making a movie called *Butch Cassidy and the Sundance Kid*, in which Etta Place, a vigorous woman with high
ideals, sets her cap for a man who understands nothing of vigor,
who turns to vapor. "If he'd pay me what he's spendin' to make
me stop robbin' him, I'd stop robbin' him." In *The Company
You Keep*, the Sundance Kid goes to meet Etta Place in a cabin
in the woods in northwest Washington, on an unnamed body
of water, but now his name is Nick and her name is Mimi and
she is played by Julie Christie. Nick needs to find Mimi: she
is the only one who can exonerate him; she knows he was not
there when the bank guard was killed. They are both living
under assumed names, but he knows where she will go, to
the cabin which once belonged to her grandfather, who is now
dead, on the island of Innisfree. Made of wattles? Yes, why not,
made of wattles. "I will arise and go now, for always night and
day / I hear lake water lapping." *Come si dice* wattles? *Bargigli*. It
is unnamed, but we—the moviegoers, Caroline, Binx Bolling,
even you—have seen it on a map. The cub reporter, intent on
his story, has found a deed in the county records office in a
small town on Puget Sound. "Who owns this?" he asks the
clerk. Dunno. He knows, we know, that the land is owned by
Mimi's family, the deed was signed by the father of a retired cop
whom the cub reporter has tracked down at a country club,

where, with the brashness of youth, for which he is too old, he
has spoken to him in menacing terms on a dock that looks out
on a covey of sailboats. Sailing is part of the history, the linked
history of the cop and Mimi. We know because we are eager. We
know the cabin floats in the landscape of dreams; it is a place
Mimi went as a child. "I know where she's headed," he says in
the movie, to a man on the telephone, whom he has also not laid
eyes on for decades. In this movie, whenever Nick shows up, a
carbon ghost, smoke still on him, someone says, "I don't need
this right now." When they were in love she brought Nick here.
We know this, we need only a few cues: the bird's-eye view, the
lens focusing on the pine trees, where Nick will go to meet Mimi,
a house which is no more a house—but the house, almost exact
in its details, where Alastair had first taken Caroline: the cabin
has an icebox on legs, a gimcrack table, white tin plates with
blue rims, a fieldstone mantel littered with a few candle stubs,
a single cot in the corner covered by a red-and-black Pendleton
blanket, a blanket that is known to Caroline, a screen door that
does not close properly. Nowhere. A house that exists on the
inside of a Japanese fan, a place you cannot see when the fan is
folded; only accessible by boat, or a passage out of time, each one
a boat journey, as is all time travel, navigated by Charon, who
is always moving between the present and the past. *Voglio una
barca mi porti lontano da qui.* "I know where she's headed," says
Butch/Nick about Etta/Mimi, his toe in the water of the dream.
The man on the telephone looks like a sharpshooter in a western,
so that the lines between the movies blur. Caroline sat in the
back so that she could keep her phone on. It was a movie she
had seen before, not this particular one but others, one where
Robert Redford played Hubbell Gardiner, a film about a love
affair that collapses under its own weight. Caroline had seen

this movie, *The Way We Were*, in which Katie Morosky is played by Barbra Streisand in a turtleneck sweater, when Caroline was quite young and had little idea of the endless permutations of the ways an ordinary house can become a smoking ruin. In *The Company You Keep*, is the man with the white beard an old friend of Butch Cassidy's, who was also on the run from the law? Was Butch Cassidy a protest movie? In what way was the protest movement like the Wild West? The fine points don't matter. In *Butch Cassidy and the Sundance Kid*, the moon rises over the flat landscape. Etta Place says, "I'll do anything you ask of me, except one thing. I won't watch you die. I'll miss that scene, if you don't mind." He is Butch, and Nick, and Hubbell Gardiner. He's also—what was his name?—Denys Finch Hatton, Paul Bratter in *Barefoot in the Park*, Bob Woodward in *All the President's Men*, and Joseph Turner in *Three Days of the Condor*. "You just keep thinking, Butch," says Sundance, "that's what you're good at."

PAUL BRATTER: You don't pick up a fork and dig into a
    black salad. You've got to play with it.

KATHY: You . . . you have a lot of very fine qualities.
    But . . .
TURNER: What fine qualities?
KATHY: You have good eyes. Not kind, but they don't lie,
    and they don't look away much, and they don't miss
    anything. I could use eyes like that.
TURNER: But you're overdue in Vermont. Is he a tough
    guy?
KATHY: He's pretty tough.
TURNER: What will he do?

KATHY: Understand, probably.
TURNER: Boy. That is tough.

BOB WOODWARD: If you're gonna hype it, hype it with
    facts. I don't mind what you did. I mind the way you
    did it.

I'll miss that scene, if you don't mind. Caroline mulls this over.
What scene would she like to miss? Perhaps Kai isn't lost, perhaps he has holed up in the cabin in the woods, under the red-
and-black Pendleton blanket? A carbon print, like the shadow
of an angel, Katie Morosky, hovered on the ceiling. "I push too
hard because I want things to be better." In the back row, with
her phone on her lap, she gave up and watched the movie.

You hum: *They laugh alike, they walk alike . . .* But how do you
know that? *We watched a lot of American TV, in Italy.* One night a
few weeks after she saw this movie, Caroline had dinner with a
friend at a place where they sat at low tables and ate bits of eel
and pork and some fried potatoes. It was late in the evening and
the streets were for once not covered with snow. There had been
a thaw, but now it was cold again. He said, "You know what I'm
tired of? I'm tired of someone saying to me, 'You are an alien
from another planet who has been sent here to destroy my life.'"

Caroline found herself snagged on this sentence. She circled it like a dog looking for a place to lie down. Often, she
would worry a phrase for days. She was indiscriminate; it could
be something she overheard, or a slogan. Skywriting. A sign on
a bus kiosk: MORE USES FOR CALCIUM! What could that mean? It
was an extremely cold night, and the wind snaked through the

door of the restaurant, which kept opening and shutting. She was wearing a pale gray shawl wrapped around her shoulders. Before she left the house, she had noticed a stain on the shawl, but it was too late to change. Too late to change, she thought. Sometimes she saw a phrase coming at her, like a gull swooping down over the sea from a great height. Meritorious. Mendacious.

*

Standing in the snow, Caroline is about four blocks from the museum, as the crow flies, where rooms that front this side of the park bear the name of a boy who drowned or disappeared, his canoe overturned, his body never found. When she was a child, she was made to rescue a life preserver from drowning again and again; it is possible, Caroline knows, to disappear. She herself is disappearing; if she stands here any longer, she will be covered in snow, a bell clapper, in her fur hat and coat and boots, a gnomon in the snow, indicating nothing. She stamps her feet.

The morning after he nicked his arm in the stand of locusts, Alastair is in a tiled bathroom on the fifth floor of his school. He is wearing the same trousers he wore the night before, and they are a little torn, but he has changed his shirt to one that Olivia, a Jamaican woman who has taken care of him since childhood and whom he loves, who "lives out" (when he heard his mother say that phrase he pictured Olivia, a massive woman, camped under a tree, in her blue uniform and carpet slippers, eating a bowl of ice cream), has washed and ironed and put on a hanger on the door of his room, and that he had folded and put in his backpack. The shirt has a small burn hole on the left front tail. His arms are itching; he has rolled up his sleeves, which he has kept rolled down and buttoned until now, and he is running his forearm, which is very white, with a few little hairs and blue veins, under the cold-water tap. He has a face painted by Perugino, sharpened by his father, who is Russian, though he is skinny still, his collarbone visible in the V-neck of his open shirt, where he has loosened his school tie. When Caroline thinks of it even now, she can feel with her lips the flat smooth planes of his face, a boy's face still visible a decade later, and remember the smell of starch and tobacco that came off his skin. She knows the loosening of that tie, the yank of it, the jerk of the wrist, the first thing he did, years later, when he loosened it, yanking it as if the tie were unbearable. Don't show off, she said to him behind the mirror, in the bathroom on Eighty-Fourth Street, coming up from behind, naked, and putting her arms around him. An aperçu, a tiny dart. They were twenty, twenty-four, twenty-six, then. Even early in the morning he smelled of gin.

In the bathroom on the fifth floor, which houses the science department—oak tables, beakers, bits of rock from the park, a bird skeleton hanging from the ceiling—Alastair is bathing his arms in water. He has been in the bathroom for five minutes. He has picked this bathroom because it is unlikely, during third period, that anyone will come in to use it. Science lab is in the afternoon. The nicks on his arm have closed overnight, but one of them is especially painful, a little deeper than the others. He gently pulls open the skin there around the cut and puts his mouth to it, and it begins to bleed again a little, into his mouth. It is disgusting and exciting. He traces the nick with his tongue. A few months later, or in the summer, the first time he puts his

mouth on the girl with the dandelion hair, opening her with his
fingers, or, her opening herself, showing him, because he knows
nothing about it yet, nothing at all, finding her with his tongue,
he thinks of the taste of his nicked arm and his tongue. And not
only that. It is 1972. A day in February. Ten years later, when
from behind Caroline put her arms around Alastair steamy from
the shower, his hand at his throat where he had just loosened his
tie, she felt the small lizard of fear, a tiny hunch, skitter across
his shoulder blades, and she put her mouth on his shoulder and
pressed it to the starched white shirt, picked up yesterday from
the Korean dry cleaner on the corner, to his skin with her lips.

A tiny hunch. The hunch of a child that has been hit. The
other night Caroline took her daughter Louie to a movie. The
movie was about a musical band of sisters, and it was showing
in the steamy theater where Caroline had lately taken herself to
see a score of movies. Louie was wearing an old skirt of Caroline's that had originally belonged to her friend Meg. It was pale
blue with tiny yellow flowers. With it she had on a silk shirt
printed with big red roses, and a pair of green lace-up boots,
much too heavy for the weather. Her hair was piled on top of
her head in the style of a 1940s telephone operator, and her face
was beautiful. When Louie was small, her skin was so white in
the winter that Caroline took her to the doctor to have her blood
checked. A snow child. Louie is tired and it is hot. When they sit
down in the movie and the credits start, she immediately begins
to weep, silent, gusty tears, and Caroline puts her arm around
her. There is no point in asking what is wrong; it is everything
and nothing. When Louie was small Caroline played tapes of
these songs to her. Why did she stop? There is something about
the songs, something treacly, something too close to the little

homemade world that Caroline tried to pull out of a hat for
her own children which now makes her recoil. Dum de-dum.
Dona nobis pacem. Instead, she puts her arm around Louie and
pulls her close. Her child smells of cigarette smoke and patch-
ouli and something else, laundry that has been left in the dryer
too long in hot weather. She pats Louie, who drives her mad.
As in so many stories, in this little movie the mother dies, or
is already dead. Louie—they are sitting in the back row of this
theater—is heaving with sobs. This is possible to do, at this theater, with no one turning around. Caroline herself has done
it. Alastair had also liked these songs; they appealed to his
sense of yearning for a childhood that never happened. As if
the little lizard did not jump. As it jumps for Caroline, and for
Louie. The lizard skittering over stones. By the pricking of my
thumbs. A childhood whose remit was nicking the roots of
the locust trees in the snow in order to dig a grave.

A few days before, Louie and Caroline had been heading
downtown on the subway, and when they changed trains Caroline got on the train and Louie did not. It had happened before.
Louie is sixteen. Caroline got off at the next station and waited
for Louie, who arrived on the next train and called her name,
stepping off the train for a moment and whisking her into it.
Louie is now in the habit of calling Caroline "Caroline," and not
Mama. It offends both of them, which is why Louie insists on
it. While Caroline waited for Louie, she held herself in check,
but when she sat down on the train she started to shake. "It's
okay," Louie said. She is a child who is incapable of the smallest
details of ordinary life but in extreme situations she is calm. She
strokes Caroline's shoulder. *It is not okay*, Caroline is thinking, *I
am capable of losing everything.*

In the winter of 1972 there is an ice storm. Ice coats every twig in the park, along Central Park West, on Riverside Drive. In her childhood house, outside Boston, it coats the trellis next to Caroline's front door. Everything cracks. When Alastair nicks the roots in the park, the ground is wet under the snow and the park is littered with broken limbs, from where the ice has snapped the branches from the elms. What Caroline does not understand about the story is that when the door opened and closed in the bathroom on the fifth floor, it made a little snapping sound, the sound of a bolt being driven home. But why would the outer door to the hall have a lock? She has asked Alastair about this, and he cannot answer her sufficiently. The other day when Caroline was at her daughter's school, in the bathroom, a school that is the "sister" school to the school Alastair attended, long ago, she looked at the interior handle of the door that opened to the hall. It is impossible for her not to look; she has looked without knowing it, a visual check, a tic, for thirty years. The door opened, it clicked shut. Perhaps simply say: *he thought it locked?*

> *And I think it's going to be a long, long time*
> *'Til touchdown brings me 'round again to find*
> *I'm not the man they think I am at home*
> *Oh, no, no, no*
> *I'm a rocket man*
> *Rocket man, burning out his fuse up here alone*

Was the bathroom door locked, or did Alastair dream it? Wouldn't he have turned around? Jean Marc Gaspard Itard, who took in the wild boy of Aveyron, whom they called Victor, said of his ability to hear noises, "Under these circumstances his ear was not an organ for the appreciation of sounds, their articulations and their combinations; it was nothing but a simple means of self-preservation which warned of the approach of a dangerous animal or the fall of wild fruit." The other day she found the contact sheets of photos of a boat, a small shipwreck by the cove, that she and Alastair photographed every day one summer and then forgot about entirely, as they forgot about everything, all projects left undone; the oaktag yellowing, a brown circle stain on it where someone had left a coffee cup. And under it a note: *I wish you wouldn't do that.* A boat barely a boat, a destination for her children, years later, every summer.

*

But what if she really is simply someone who waits in the doorway staring up at a lit window, that that is why you chose her, because you knew that; and she chose you because you knew, and her refusal to be that person is—sheer bloody-mindedness? You are doing what you do, and walking away, and talking about things that have no answer: stay in the bathroom with Alastair. *I'd rather skip that scene, if you don't mind.* Stay there. In the bathroom, Alastair has the cold tap running; he is watching the water swirl down the metal drain. In Australia, he knows, the water goes down the other way. *Widdershins.* From Old German: against, contrary. From *sind*: journey, to send. Can the wrong way be the start of a journey? And once you started, was there no way to head back? One foot in front of the other: the sound of bells, ice cracking, water jangling in the basin, blood beating in Alastair's temples, a tiny boat made of paper, tipped.

Caroline is sitting in bed in July at seven in the morning about forty years after Alastair heard the door open and close in the bathroom, looking out on fields full of lilies in a place she loves as much as she loves anywhere in the world: a house in the country that belongs to a friend. Yesterday when she arrived, she discovered she had forgotten her hat, but in the kitchen she found a pink sun hat printed with flowers which she left at the house years ago, which has hung on the hook since, and put it on instead. The brim flops. It is a silly hat. Alastair has written to her—it was her birthday yesterday. Also, a message from a friend who years ago married the girl whom Alastair left when he fell in love with Caroline. *Where are you?* Caroline replied. This morning at six a.m. he replied, *In situ*. The day they were married was very hot. Caroline was there with her first husband. She wore a blue watered-silk dress with an Indian print which had belonged to her mother. It was tight around the waist and later tore. The wedding took place at an estate that had belonged to Toscanini but was now a public garden. Her mother had been there as a girl, she had dated Toscanini's grandson, Wally. To Caroline the name Wally conjures up a playwright, who is an acquaintance of hers. The other night, really not very long ago, perhaps two weeks ago, she went to see a play of his. During the performance, the man she was with very slowly stroked her shoulder, under the cap sleeve of her black dress. The play was called *The Designated Mourner*. The man, who was Wally but is called Jack, says to Deborah, who is his girlfriend or wife—who knows?—in real life but in the play is called Judy, "Look, I've tried to tell you about myself, about what I'm like, over the years, but your mind, apparently, has always been somewhere else, unfortunately . . ." And Judy, who is Deborah, says, "Can't I be saved?" We saw that play together, you and I.

Yes? And we went downstairs to the concession stand at the in-
termission and you did not want sugar in your tea. Later, much
later, or was it earlier, Caroline would fall in love with a childhood friend of the playwright, and that love would or would not
save her, but that is another story. For now, the sun is streaming
through the window above the fields of lilies. Caroline needs to
stay in that bathroom with Alastair, she cannot leave him; she
is, for Alastair, the designated mourner.

*

*An ant skirts the boards of the porch, measuring the distance between
them, up and down, a foot from the dark imbroglio of the screen
door. An ant with a body like three barrels. Beyond, in the field, the
jimsonweed is higher than the ferns. Where the planks, weathered,
kitten brown, are nailed to the strut below—silver nailheads in single
file—the boards are slightly closer together, and the ant found it could
make the crossing, one half of its body straddling the lurch between
the boards. The ant is thinking it through, she thought. The ant was
joined by another. They had been going up and down the planks. Now
they crossed over. The sky had darkened and the ferns were neon
green. The foreground was accentuated, louder, hard on the eye. It
was exhausting. She shut her eyes for a moment, but her lids were
hot. Last night as she walked along the road, her light wavering, like
a flying saucer in the trees, fireflies. One, then another, gems. She
had learned the name in Italian, lucciola. A word for streetwalker
She was walking on the road with her flashlight and she turned it off.
The fireflies in a dome above the field, fixed as constellations, a ring
around the rose, circling the earth. Once, in Montalcino the fireflies
were on one side of the road, but not the other (was it the grapes they
liked, or olives, she couldn't remember), and then, there they were*

again, twenty years later, last summer, like spawn lighting the pasture, as she looked out the window past the lilies. How beautiful, she had said. But did not turn to where James stood beside her, a cousin of the house, whom she had known since the years between them made him a child and her older than she was, really. She had always liked him. The moment passed when she could have said—what? And one or two fireflies lighting the garden, like Sargent's Japanese lanterns, goldfish swimming in a blue-green bowl. Last year someone had said, looking over the garden, But I could sit here forever. Last night at the bonfire, she had fed a name to the fire. Beyond the porch, the plastic lawn chair is a smear of turquoise blue, greenish mold on the strap, the color of a slide of penicillin. Now the sun came out from a cloud and took the glamour from the ferns. Unruly sun, and then? Two people, at a table, a bat beating the curtain. Not so much tired—and here she shook her head at herself, as she would straighten her hat in the mirror—as afraid.

For what good did it do? The smell of charred wood came through the trees. Last night at the bonfire a man—a man whom she disliked, his voice booming, going on—had burned a cello. He had put it in the fire. It was terrible, she thought. She had only heard about it in the morning, standing on the steps, before going into town. An old cello. She had never thought to wonder what became of old instruments. Perhaps it had not been very valuable, or valuable at all. But it seemed terrible. The man had struck her as someone who would make much of things other people would leave be. A fire starter. But then, she had put a name into the fire. The wedding was tomorrow. She had said she would go. It was a spell: if she did not promise, she would not go. A book in which she might be absent from a chapter. But she would go.

*

She doesn't want to stay in the bathroom, where the story is written in hieroglyphs in the old black-and-white Moorish tile, in the silver marks on the mirrors. The thought of it exhausts her. As Etta says, "I'd rather skip that scene, if you don't mind." She is Gerda in the town square, the snow falling, listening to the bells in the wake of Kai's . . . disappearance. She knows he has disappeared. She knows that her life will be organized around his disappearance; she does not realize that in this . . . Quonset hut of the past . . . she herself will vanish, drawn through that needle, a knotless thread. In the bathroom the water is ice-cold. Alastair has plugged the basin so that he can keep his nicked arm under the water; the old yellowed rubber stopper is connected to the tap by a metal chain. Someone has written NERD YOU SUCK in black indelible magic marker in the upper left-hand corner of the mirror above the sink. Alastair registers vaguely that the letters have been there for months. *Who sucks?* The question trails above his head like the banner pulled by a prop plane in the summer above the field in Maine where he plays baseball, half a mile from the house that belonged to his grandfather to which he would take Caroline nine years later, pulling her jeans down around her ankles and leaving them there, so that when she woke at three a.m. she would trip getting up. What did the skywriting say? *Drink Budweiser, Kreemo Toffee, You Are Annihilating Me.* In the mirror Alastair shuts his eyes, his cut arm twisted behind him, the mirror blurring the black letters, the rowan branches with their serrated leaves.

In real time, that is, right now, or—not exactly—last night, in New York, Caroline received an email from Alastair in response to one she had written the night before, to a note he had written six weeks previously which she had not answered. The beginning of hers read, *And now it is me who has taken a long time to reply, but between us does it matter?* Alastair replied, *I want to say to your first sentences that it is just a very slow and careful game of ping-pong, maybe the kind played with zero gravity, or very little gravity, like a game on Mars . . . and I guess we would know if the message said, Come now, which is what I say to the dog when he chases a horse. You are not drowning, are you?* She thinks it over. No, she is not drowning.

He did not take off his shirt for two years. That summer he rubbed his arms with poison ivy so that blisters started up, and he kept his shirt on while swimming and playing ball, because the sun would make the poison ivy worse, and when the blisters subsided, he reinfected himself by rolling in the patch of ivy beyond the shed. The reaction was worse the second time and the third. Because he had poison ivy all his towels had to be washed. He washed his own clothes and he never touched anyone. By the summer the welts on his back where the leather had scored his flesh had healed enough that he did not bleed on the sheets. Once, he had bled onto a beautiful white shirt he had been told to put on. The second summer it was done, but he continued to wear a dark blue New York Mets T-shirt, and he was used to the poison ivy. Forty years later a man in a dim room who encouraged him to stop drinking (you are annihilating yourself) said, "What could they have been thinking?" "Who?" asked Alastair. About what? A knock-knock joke. Knock-knock. Who's there? To. To who? To whom. An owl in the branches of the pine above the house, the field rimmed with fireflies.

The last time Caroline saw Alastair was July 1987, on Central Park West, at the corner of Seventy-Second Street. That is, the last time she saw him before, years later, she saw him again. When he came back from Somalia that summer, a country to which she had refused to go, a country which in all probability she will never visit, she had gone to meet him in a house that was then still owned by his grandfather, near the house where she had slept tangled on the rug before the fire. The wallpaper in the bedroom was printed with little buckets filled with flowers. There were bees in the walls and wasps in the bathroom, the paint was coming off the window sashes, and it smelled of damp. When Caroline was very young she knew a man whose face had been scarred by a fire when he was a boy; after she had known him awhile, she did not notice the taut purplish burn that marked half his face.

Alastair's back was like that? Yes. But this is what you have not told me: What did he tell his parents? He told them that while he was staying with his friend Tobias in the country, he had been thrown by a horse onto a barbed-wire fence. They believed that? Yes. A man who was hurt and lost and disappeared and then was rescued. Many years after Caroline and Alastair spent a week in his grandfather's cottage—a week in which they barely left the house, although she sometimes sat on the little rise of lawn and read stories of men and women in love, intensely, as though if she read carefully enough, the text would teach her something (they were Irish stories, and tended to end in death or heartbreak, and often both)—she went to an opening at an art gallery with the man to whom she was then married. To whom she is still married, although they have not lived together for years. The art gallery was part of a school, and because her husband had been involved in curating this show—prints between the wars, or English watercolors of India, she cannot remember—they were put up in a guesthouse that belonged to the school. In the bedroom of the house the wallpaper was covered with flowers in buckets. The day before, if she had been asked to describe the wallpaper at Alastair's grandfather's house, she would not have been able to bring it to mind—she had not thought of that house for almost thirty years—but when she walked into the room, the skin on her arms began to burn and the room to spin. They had stayed for a week; after three or four days, the walls had started to disintegrate around them. Dishes were left in the sink, the curtains sucked up stains, the milk went bad, mold bloomed in the shower, at night the sheets wound themselves around her legs as Alastair, his breath on her neck, held her so tightly she could not breathe. It was as if the house had turned itself inside out and there was nothing for it—it did not occur to Caroline to try to whack back the clothes and laundry on the floor while Alastair lay weeping on the sofa.

What is the truth, still? The truth is that she has never yet loved anyone the way she loves Alastair. Or loved Alastair. It makes no difference; it doesn't matter what you say today or tomorrow. Alastair lay weeping on the sofa, his back heaving. In the bathroom two clouds of condensation bloomed on the glass. Feverfew spackled the sun-splotched lawn outside the door. Thirty years later in the snow by the locust trees, where the scar on the roots of the tree made by a boy hacking at them with a penknife has grown over, knobby as a ginger root, white-knuckled, not even Alastair would be able to find the exact tree, where forty or two hundred years ago, a sheep, or was it a boy who could not speak, was caught in a barbed-wire fence by the road meant to keep it from straying. This is what Alastair told his mother, yes? Yes.

*

In a hotel room in Minneapolis, where it is snowing, Caroline put on her coat in order to go to supper before a performance of *Peer Gynt*. When Gerda leaves her grandmother and the warm oven where the cookies are baking for tea—shortbread cookies in the shape of hearts, Gerda has cut them out herself—for when Kai will return, as he always does, to sit with them, she puts on her jacket, a red jacket with roses embroidered on the pockets, and a red hat and goes out to look for him. Although she does not know she has heard it, the jingle of the Snow Queen's sled has snagged her heart. It circles her and pulls her out the door, a corset of wire, which she feels tightening, as if her heart is caged. When Gerda's father was alive, he would take her out in a sailboat in the harbor and tell her to listen for the scream of the wind in the rigging. A banshee. The jangle of the Snow Queen's sled sounded like that scream, a banshee pierced by knives, like the Ten of Swords in the tarot pack. Once upon a time there was a little girl who had a blue jacket with an orange lining with a hood, and on the back and on the pockets were embroidered scenes of a bear family, with a jar of honey and a bee. The bee's body was yellow and white and black, the size of a fingernail. The moon rises over the flat landscape. Etta Place says, "I'll do anything you ask of me except one thing. I won't watch you die. I'll skip that scene, if you don't mind." A story folded inside a story, folding itself smaller and smaller, until it is no bigger than a speck of salt. A cinder. But the extraordinary thing about crumpled paper is that the creases are always the same length. How unwise it is to look back. But it is all we know, the pictures hanging in our little hut of time.

*

When Alastair came back from Somalia, in the middle of the week they spent together, in the house with the overturned buckets of flowers and mold growing up the shower curtain, he had fallen in love. That is the word he used? Yes. Her name was Mona. She was sixteen. Maybe seventeen. Or she told him she was seventeen and he pretended to believe it. She was the eldest of seven children. Improbably she spoke English. She was so thin that her elbows were white under her skin. Because she was—what, because nothing, he felt terrible about leaving her, she was now living in the house he had found in Mogadishu, on money he had left with her, five hundred dollars, a huge sum. He needed, he said, to go back. Caroline folded this thought, so light and fine, a girl like a star, a shard in the corner of her eye, and put it in a walnut shell. They had arrived on Sunday. By Thursday the wallpaper with the strewn baskets of dried flowers had begun to peel off the walls. She got into the car, an old station wagon which had belonged to her father, and left. A week or so later, she called him, but the phone rang and rang and he did not pick up. She saw him once after that, on a bench on Central Park West. It was September, a month or so later. Somewhere in her body Caroline remembers getting up from the bench and turning to go, in her knees a little tension. A lizard skittering. She was wearing a pale blue skirt printed

with yellow buds. What if someone had said to her then, You
will not see Alastair again for twenty-three years?

You pick up your head. You say: You have left her in the
park, when you said you would not wait in a doorway! She is
still standing there! I said I would not wait for you, in your doorway. But you did! You did! You have left Caroline in the snow:
you have left two characters standing around! Say the rest of
what happened so we can move on. You are teaching yourself
something; what is it? Kindness, perhaps. Let's learn that.

*

Caroline is in the snow in her fur boots and hat. In her hand,
inside her glove, is a cell phone. She has turned it to vibrate and
she is waiting for Alastair to call her. She is freezing, despite her
fur coat and hat. She is cold, like Little Bear, a fictional bear,
whom she loved as a child, about whom she read to her children. When she grew up, she befriended—although that is not
exactly the right word—the man who drew the illustrations for
Little Bear, who made the picture of Little Bear she has in her
head, but that was later. Was that person Caroline? I think so.
Now be quiet. It is snowing and Little Bear, who lives in a very
nice hut in the woods with his mother, Mother Bear, goes outside to play. Her name is Mother Bear? Hush. He is outside for
about two minutes, and then he comes back inside and says to
his mother, "Mother Bear, I am cold. See the snow. I want something to put on." She gives him a hat. Two minutes later, the
scene is repeated, and she makes him a jacket and snow pants,
and so on. He goes in and out. Finally, he asks for a fur coat.
But, says Mother Bear, "You have your own fur coat!" Little Bear

takes off the hat, the jacket, and the snow pants, goes outside, in his own fur coat, into the snow. Well, that has every element Caroline likes: someone dressing and undressing someone else. She's his mother! Little Bear is *born* with a fur coat, how lovely. Did you have a mother? You had a mother and not a father, and I had a father but not a mother. Which is worse?

Caroline is standing in the snow in her fur hat and fur boots waiting for Alastair to call, a few yards from where thirty years before he hacked at the frozen roots of a locust tree with his penknife, and cut his arm. The next day he went back to school and washed his arm in the basin, and ten or twelve years ago Caroline would walk away from him as he sat on a park bench on Central Park West, on a warm day in August 1986. Or was it September 1987? She would have two daughters, Louie and Pom, and a son, George. Are those their real names? No. Alastair looked in the mirror and Caroline turned her face away from the mirror, which was wreathed with rowan. But there are some mirrors that will not relinquish a gaze. And then he could not tear himself away, is that how you say it in English? Yes. He could not tear himself away. He could not tear himself away, because his arms were bound to his sides. And neither can you. No. Neither can I.

Caroline is standing in her fur hat and boots, in February. A child stands in the vestibule inside a stand of boxwood. She has made the boxwood house herself; she hides things under a stone—a muddy book, a shoelace. When she tells a story to herself, the long-winded story of her love for Alastair, she embroiders it and then rips it apart, angrily, as one would rip, in exasperation, at a shirt that is stuck on a zipper, or a button,

yanking it and tearing the cloth. A hasty gesture, instantly regretted. A sentiment she expressed, in tears, sitting on the side
of the road where she had pulled the car into a lay-by: I know
this feeling, and it has your name on it. Or perhaps she said: I
remember. It was a month after she began speaking, again, to
Alastair. Because speaking was a way of remembering, as if a
part of Caroline had come alive again—a phantom limb. By the
pricking of my thumbs.

There are ways that Caroline resembles her father, who is
an autocrat, and one of them is her inability to let anything go.
Her father will and will not let her go. The only time that Caroline's father, who is now an old man, has ever raised ordinary
matters of mortality with her was to discuss the dispensation
of his estate should she die before he does. For months after this
conversation, which took place in a diner on Broadway, Caroline
tried to imagine a similar conversation with one of her children,
in which they sat together eating grilled cheese sandwiches and
drinking coffee from thick mugs and imagined a scenario in
which that child is dead. Once, she had a conversation with her
husband, to whom she was then still married, on a subway car,
in which he told her that he hoped he could receive a letter from
her as full of love as the letter Virginia Woolf left for her husband
when she drowned herself in the River Ouse. She has wondered
at this propensity to imagine her death.

> What I want to say is I owe all the happiness of my life to
> you. You have been entirely patient with me and incredibly
> good. I want to say that—everybody knows it. If anybody
> could have saved me it would have been you.

When she was first married she lived in an apartment where the icebox leaked. In the freezer for reasons completely unknown or forgotten there was a lightbulb stowed in the door. Caroline became superstitious about this lightbulb. She was sure if it was moved or thrown away or taken out of its long coma in the deep freeze, things would begin to fall apart. The lightbulb, ridiculous in the freezer, a little frozen planet, was the eye at the center of the drawstring bag, the cold light in the center of the black hole of the universe in which everything else was kept: supper, the children, the pull toys they had, checkbooks and bath salts, missing keys, erasers, barrettes, shells picked up at the beach which needed to be soaked in bleach and vinegar so they did not smell, but were not, so that the hallway in the fall when they returned to the beach smelled like the tide going out. Was she right? It is hard to know, when things begin to fall apart. Once, in a fury she said to the man who became her second husband, "All the men who loved me still love me, only you don't." And he said, "They didn't marry you."

*

When Caroline first heard from Alastair, she was in the laundry room. Then, there was a telephone in the basement. Since then that telephone has been disconnected; there is a bookshelf that blocks the outlet, but then it was attached to the wall by a long cord. The house was rebuilt just long enough ago that some of the telephones have wires by which the receiver is attached to the cradle. There was a discussion about it at the time; Caroline did not want only cordless phones: the children will answer the telephones, she said, and then leave the receivers around and we will not be able to find them. This is what happened; the cordless receivers were always missing, but it was impossible in any case to make a call from a wall phone if there was a receiver off the hook somewhere else.

Caroline is standing in the snow in her fur hat and fur boots waiting for Alastair to call, a few yards from the vanished locust trees. Now it is later in the evening and I am typing at night— I am beginning to feel that time is running out, and that I am running after a light in the dark, the way you might run after a car, helplessly, which is rolling down the drive, illuminating the boxwood with its headlights, green bright against the black. Running behind something or someone that is leaving forever. Louie is singing upstairs. She is seventeen and she is leaving for Italy in two days on a Lufthansa flight that leaves at ten in the evening from Boston. She is singing, alternately, "Dona Nobis Pacem" and "Boots of Spanish Leather." She sings beautifully, her voice sliding down the steep banister, in this house, which is three hundred years old but is free of ghosts, as if it had been swept clean. But I feel I must finish before—before I leave. Stop counting everything up, accounting. This one so much, this one so much. Louie has come downstairs.

*

She had shown the scar, a fingernail moon on her knee, to Louie and Pom. So much blood! She had one other, in the web between her left thumb and forefinger. Thirty, forty years ago. Even now she can feel the silvery hump under the skin, like a sheet wrinkled under a coverlet. Sunday morning. They are in bed with her. Why, oh why must they dig up the road, even on Sunday, with that terrible noise? And now the sun is too hot. There is the bird again, in the shade, the steel sound of a row of triangles rung all at once. Outside, birdsong dips into the ferns, which are spotted here and there with white flowers, like a ladle into the Milky Way. She thinks of James watching the fireflies, and the dry thunderstorm fires in Portugal. A tree struck by lightning. A photograph of James as a child, in the Borghese gardens, with a lion beside him. Is this possible? There is the picture. In the garden here, the wax flowers of the Solomon's seal, the coral bells, the ajuga veined with lavender, the pumpkin vine. It is on her bureau, he sent it to her. But now he is a man in a white shirt, in Italy, reading a guidebook, ordering his lunch in a restaurant. There, said her mother, dabbing at her knee.

She had fallen from the high, sharp curb into the slick of oil-spattered water, the colors running so that later when she first saw the marbleized papers in Florence, she felt a stab of pain. She fell on a sharp piece of glass. She had been walking with her father and mother, who had swung her down past the curb, but she had slipped, her knee buckling, her red shoe breaking the water. Her father had taken charge. Her father in his unbelted raincoat, swinging her up, so broad she could not take him in, the breadth of him, the smell of his stiff white shirt from the Chinese laundry, his tie, crooked now, the knot slightly loose, printed with small medallions as if he had won a game fought by tiny players. She thought of a mournful nod of gray heads, a hangman's council in the hat trial, Bartholomew Cubbins's hats discarded one after another, a story she had learned to read herself, and that she would sit and read to Louie in the armchair, the very same copy, see, there is Mama's name written on the flyleaf, a story which ended with a cocked hat embellished with a glittering jewel, the shape of one medallion. Louie crossed out her name and wrote her own, under it: This book belongs to Louie. *Just like that, with one stroke, her name, gone.*

Four doors down, there was a pharmacy on the corner, the plate glass illuminated like a fish tank in the rain, half a block from the curb where she fell on the serpent's slick tail, the rainbow slipping into the gutter. A shimmy of bells at the door. Inside it was warm and light and the rain had stopped. A smell—was it formaldehyde?—thick and metallic, a porch-screen smell, her nose pressed up against it, her eyes closed, then open, gazing at the cupped leaves of the boxwood. Her father wore a tweed jacket under his raincoat, his gray trousers—he was wearing a hat, with a blue band. Her knee dangled as he held her tightly against his chest, awkwardly, a man unused to carrying children but who could do anything, a man in America, accustomed to opening the doors of shops in which his patronage was desired, who would be seen to immediately by the pharmacist who wore a white coat over his shirt and tie. Her father swung her up on a table. "In a jiffy," said her mother. A siren had arrived—she was screaming now, the sound high up in her throat. Her black serge tights had been stripped, her mother held her legs, the pharmacist, a man unknown to her, who smelled of what she would later identify as death, the stench of hospital corridors, swabbed a brown solution the color of peat on her ravaged knee, the bloody place the serpent had bit. "Good girl," he said.

Her father nodded as if the pharmacist, the stranger, had been speaking to him. Implicit in each of her father's actions was: every word is, must be, addressed to him. A man who had a horror of dirt, who would not drink a glass of water from the bathroom faucet. When he came to her house when she was a grown woman, with children, where the piano sat in the hall, the piano that had been his mother's, and the portrait of the piano and his mother, and himself as a small boy at her feet, was hanging on the upstairs landing—he would have had this portrait thrown out, for he was never a small

boy—he would say very quietly to Pom or Louie that the knife wasn't
quite clean, quietly, so as not to draw attention. But never to George,
for what business of it was his, forks and knives and spoons? A man
who, when he met an acquaintance in the street, clapped him on the
shoulder, the smile lingering on his face long after. Now there was a
piece of gauze on her knee, and a square bandage; the tape made a
square. "What did the little bird say?" her father said. During the
week he was almost never home. Her mother kept his dinner warm
on a special tray. "Chirrup, chirrup," said her father, and swung her
off the table. The bird chiming in the wood.

A hundred, a thousand years ago, she fell from the curb. Now,
beyond the lilies, the afternoon light, pooling in the trees. The four-
o'clocks open, purple and green. Her watch is fast, its rubbed red
leather strap is too big, it turns the face to the inside of her wrist. Yesterday, a man pointed into the tree: look, a raven. A crow darted and
chased it. Because it was midsummer, there had been a bonfire in the
wood, the flames the color of the lilies at the side of the road, swaths
of them in June, the embers spiraling up the ratcheted branches, like
the wings of monarch butterflies. Ridiculous, but it was beautiful. She
would remember it. The one person, gruff against the night sky with
the small crescent moon, to whom she would have spoken not talking
to her. The crescent moon moved into the raven's nest. She was too old.
A man had put a cello into a fire. The rainbow sky slithered to the very
edge of the field, to the horizon. The sun so long up in the sky had set.
The crescent moon rose, a rent in the sky's black serge stocking. When
she was a girl, she'd bit her fingernails until the skin bled. Stop it, her
mother said. Now she batted Pom's hand away from her mouth. At
the bonfire, a game: a sheaf of paper and a pencil in a basket. A little
bird told me. Silly, she thought, and missed Pom looking for her in the

dark. I must, she thought, I must. And she wrote a name on a piece of paper and threw it into the fire. It made no difference.

*

Caroline is standing in the snow in her fur boots and hat. It is February. It is exactly halfway between the time she saw Alastair again, the previous November, after twenty-five years, and when she would see him for the last time, the following November. (But this isn't exactly true, is it? She saw him again.) In her fur hat and boots, she is frozen, a bubble in a spirit level made of ice. Her eyes are green.

That was the color of your eyes when you came back from Italy. It doesn't matter what color my eyes were. Caroline is in the laundry room; Caroline is in the snow; which is it? When the phone rang in the basement, the telephone that is now disconnected, it was Colin, to whom she had not spoken in months. Alastair's father was dead. Did she want to go to the funeral, which was that weekend, in Maine? It was not a funeral but a memorial service. *I'd rather skip that scene, if you don't mind.* Caroline skipped that scene, although she considered it; a black hat and veil, Lea Massari, her face in shadow, reappearing twenty-five years after she vanished in the Aeolian islands, like a gust of air, an apocryphal tale; a future that tells us a truth about the past, as if we did not already know. But she asked for Alastair's email address and wrote a formal note of sympathy to the address she was given, an office email, at the small consulting firm where he worked. She also wrote to his mother, but did not receive a reply. Alastair replied.

After two or three formal notes, back and forth, Alastair
wrote to Caroline that he loved her and loved her still. Not a
day went by when he did not think of her. Caroline was not
quite sure who she is now, sitting in her pink sun hat in the
garden, but still, it amused her. But the more she thought about
it, the less she found it amusing. She was unhappy, she had not
known how unhappy she was. She was unhappy because she
had left Alastair, who pictured her with her hair around her
shoulders, down to her waist, wearing a black leather miniskirt,
with her bitten nails. Because by now the Internet had been
invented, Caroline and Alastair began to exchange letters. He
also taught her how to chat on the computer, a feat that took
many nights and led to a great deal of exasperation, a mode
which made them happy as it was familiar to them. She sat up
late in her nightgown staring at the blue screen, a pool willing
him to appear, which he did, talking to her in tongues. She had
refused to look in the mirror wreathed with rowan leaves;
now she sat looking at the screen. Caroline was never sure
whether she dove down or the rising pool of slick water caught
her up. She put a toe in the water and the water ignited, like
gasoline on the surface of a pond, that beautiful sharp-toothed
rainbow, and caught her, and she fell or was incorporated into
the flame and turned to carbon. He swept her up.

Years ago, when she learned to type, back when that was a
special skill, she was taught to use carbon paper to save a copy
of a typed letter. The little hammers of the typewriter, each bear-
ing its stamp, branded the sheet of blue-black; a copy looked
like a copy—the letters always faintly smeared, numinous: an
afterimage on the retina. Caroline knew from the start that she

was writing to a ghost: she knew, too, that she was a ghost writing to a ghost.

During their midnight conversations, Caroline sat up late in her study, while her children slept upstairs—a room that is now unused, except as a gigantic closet, in which clothes she will most likely never wear again are strewn over the chairs and even the table, as if the closet had exploded—Caroline learned a good deal about Alastair. He did not sleep with his wife but in a room over the garage, on a sofa, with his dog. The room had a large sliding glass door that opened over a field. The glass was insulated. His dog was called Angus. She was shown a picture of his sister, who had been a beauty, a woman now encased in what looked like an extra suit of clothes, although Caroline could still find her face, the face of a sleeping child. His brother, Otto, now ran a plumbing company. His father had died slowly of liver cancer; Alastair had often been called by his mother, whom he loathed, in the middle of the night, as this dying took place at home. When she tried to picture Alastair's father, whom she had loved, she saw a man in shadow in a blue room lit by a bedside lamp, while outside the window it was snowing. Alastair's grandmother, who chastised Caroline many years ago, clutching her arm in the kitchen, was dead.

After a week or two of exchanges Alastair wrote to her from a different email. It was one he used, occasionally, he said. It would be better if they continued writing to each other using this address. It did not occur to her that a secret email address is a warning sign, a little red light. For her part, she continued to use the email address she had always used, although she changed the password. Caroline, who is naïve, and obtuse, and likes repetition, because *you can see where you are*, even if you are walking the plank, failed to see that people who have secret email addresses are perhaps not entirely dependable. In this new email box, Alastair spoke to Caroline. It was like whispering under the blankets, two children talking together. They were back in the place they had been before they were interrupted. He held her shoulder in his hand. He latched his finger on her clavicle. She needed only the sound of his voice, which was audible under the commas and phrasing of his sentences, to feel this. This is something that she hears: Your knee fits my hand, your breast fits my hand, my hand fits perfectly, there, on your hip. Perhaps everyone hears this.

One of the things he told her was that he spent a lot of time, in the room over the garage, on the Internet. He mentioned this casually. She thought, *Well, I am spending a lot of time on the Internet, talking to you. Lizard's leg and owlet's wing*—it was early days. She did not spend time on the Internet, generally. She envisioned it as a vast galaxy, filled with tiny stars, like fizz or carbonation. At night in the summer she would take the children to the head of the dune, and they would watch the Pleiades in a dark velvet sky. Until recently, she had not owned a computer. Her father had communicated to her many times, culminating in a letter typed by his secretary on his letterhead, that she was condemning her children to lives of menial work, as their peers would be flying right by them into lucrative careers. She had caved, as her children phrased it, when her father offered to buy her a dishwasher if she allowed him to buy the children a computer. Now the house had three computers, and one of them was in her study. The curtains in the study, drawn at night, were silk patterned with green leaves and rickshaws. The screen was a mirror.

I was in my twenties . . . One day I was on a small boat with some people from a fishing family. While we were waiting to shoot the nets, an individual known as Petit-Jean pointed out something floating on the surface of the waves. It was a small can, a can of sardines . . . It shone in the sun. And Petit-Jean said to me—You see the can? Well, it doesn't see you.

Did Alastair and Caroline see each other? Do they now? One of Caroline's tactics when at a loss, or pretending to be at a loss, was to conduct her interior life in the open. To hide in plain sight. What Caroline knew without being able to say it aloud, without even thinking it, was that for Alastair the Internet, which he entered through the blue screen, late at night, was the mirror he had looked into when he washed the blood from his cuts in the fifth-floor bathroom of the school. It was the same blue as the flickering televisions of their childhoods, when to order a lamp, a handy cooler, a guaranteed weight-loss plan, a fire ladder made of rope you could keep in your child's second-floor bedroom for when disaster strikes, as it will, you called MUrray Hill 7-7500. Hello there. On the Internet, he told her, he was known as ——. Caroline cannot remember it now, the name. When she tries to think of it, the tips of her fingers grow numb. When he told her this, she knew that she had known all along.

What did she know? The reason rowan leaves are not brought into the house is that they smell of the dead. Caroline, who as a child would not look in the mirror, did not look now; instead, she looked down into the pool in which Alastair was swimming. *You see the can? Well, it doesn't see you.* What language is the language spoken in the icy pool? There is no language. It has worn off the keys, the water lapping has worn it away. Because she had known it all along, she continued to move through the months with the certainty of someone in a dream.

By November they had made a plan, because Caroline had insisted. They decide, writing to each other late at night, conspirators, they will meet in November. This involves complicated arrangements, not surprisingly. For one thing, the house in Maine, where they plan to meet, is shut up for the winter. For another, if it snows hard, the road may be impassable. What kind of car do you have now? Alastair asks. Caroline tells him. Probably okay, he says. It is the first normal conversation they have had. Ordinary. When Kai disappears into the frozen wood from the town square, Gerda—once she discovers he has gone—follows him. Caroline had not thought about Alastair for many years, except in dreams in which she was on a bus going to see him but traveling in the wrong direction, and the conductor would not accept her ticket, dreams in which she was both calling him on the telephone, the black coil connecting her to the phone box, and not picking up the phone in the house that she was calling—a thwarted call-and-response, in which she quite literally hung up on herself. She did not know that Alastair was lost. He was lost to her, but that is something else. But he was not lost, no? He was somewhere else, as Kai was somewhere—it is to Gerda that he is lost, and it's hard to know what Kai thinks of the story. His voice is silent. The story is Gerda's. That is true. And this is Caroline's story. Yes and no.

Tu chiedi se così tutto vanisce
in questa poca nebbia di memorie . . .

*

They had made a plan, because Caroline had insisted. Caroline likes plans, yes? She does. It is a mistake. Maybe. But *Honour thy error as a hidden intention.* In the movies, where she sat in the back row and waited for the phone to ring—by then, she was not waiting for Alastair, by then she was waiting for you to call; she is always waiting because that means she does not have to decide for herself—Mimi and Nick (who look familiar to Caroline—where has she met them?) meet in a house that the young reporter has found by looking at old title maps; that's where they are, he says. Mimi will need to escape, but Caroline on the contrary did not want to get out; on the contrary she wanted nothing more than to be there, in the woods, in a place of what used to be called "grave danger."

By early November they had made a plan. It was Caroline who insisted on it. She wanted to see him; this as it turned out took some doing; it is hard to bring someone back from the land of the dead. One afternoon in November she cut short a class she was teaching and drove north. She was wearing blue trousers and a green silk shirt, a shearling coat, and a black cashmere scarf. No hat? Where was her hat? It doesn't matter where she left her hat! (It always matters.)

It was snowing. When she passed Boston, she undid her hair, which was pinned to her head. By three p.m. it was almost dark. She drove too fast, and wildly. She went through the cash toll rather than using E-ZPass, and she paid cash for gas in a station off the highway near Amherst.

Was she behaving like a fugitive? Yes, like a fugitive. Or like a ghost. When she shut the door of the car, she entered the place which is no place, between ago and again. She told no one where she was going. Because she had not been to the house for almost twenty-five years, and when she was there she had been someone else, or at least that's what she thought, not who she is now, her mind felt wiped clean, as if she had just enough vocabulary to order a sandwich that she will not eat, to ask the time but without syntax. A life sentence without syntax is hard to manage. What are words? asked her English teacher Mr. O'Rourke, brandishing the white chalk against the blackboard. From the time Caroline was a child, she'd had a re-curring dream: she was looking at a page she had written, and she could not read it. Mr. O'Rourke's handwriting looped across the empty night sky of the blackboard, the curving letters bow-ing their necks like swans. *Rose is a rose is a rose*, he wrote. *So we beat on, boats against the current, borne back ceaselessly into the past. How do you like your blue-eyed boy, Mister Death? Been down so long it looks like up to me. Positively Fourth Street.*

Was it typed or handwritten? Sometimes it is typed, and sometimes it is handwritten. The page is a pool, she is swim-ming between the lanes of type. A girl in a blue bathing suit. A few days before she drove north, she bought a map of Maine in a bookstore. It was snowing, and she was waiting in the bookstore, which does not exist anymore, that bookstore on the corner of Broadway and Lafayette, where you went upstairs? Yes, I remember it. She was waiting for her husband. They were meeting friends for dinner. Caroline went upstairs to the second floor of the shop and stood by the bookcase that held the shop's small collection of poetry titles. She had not picked up a book of poetry for eight years. For eight years? Yes. For the sorcerer, you know, eight is a dangerous number because it is infinite. It turns back on itself. *Ago and Again.*

It is a little pretentious, you think, this bit about Caroline at the bookshelf? Yes, but that is how it happened. Caroline was standing by the bookshelf, and she pulled out a copy of the *Duino Elegies* and read the third elegy in German and burst into tears. She does not read German. She reads Rilke. Her husband is late. Here is a word I just learned, *afficordo*. If she knows something by heart, does she need to be able to read the original language? No, she does not. That is how she can talk to you. She is learning how by heart. By ear? No, she has no ear. When she went down to meet her husband, she hid the map of Maine inside the Rilke which had spoken to her from the shelf. She thought, *Now, it starts.* Her husband was a person who is always late, who is never waiting for someone else to arrive.

Before Caroline went to meet Alastair, he sent her directions: she could not remember how to get from the center of town to the house, which was five miles away. In subsequent meetings, she would leave her car in the parking lot of the Hannaford off exit 28, but they did not think of this the first time, although it turned out he was worried that someone would see her car. He did not tell her this. She drove through the falling snow on the interstate and crossed into Maine. Near the state line, there was a welcome center, and she pulled off the highway. A white-haired woman was wearing a blue cardigan over a white turtleneck printed with ladybugs. *Ladybug, ladybug, fly away home, your house is on fire, your children will burn.* There was a rack of pamphlets: SEE SCENIC MAINE. Caroline had a map. The woman looked concerned when she walked in. Why? Because she looked like a madwoman. She looked like a person who is lost. At the welcome center, she went to the bathroom. In the stall she took off her coat and held it on her lap. She had lost so much weight that she could take off her trousers without unbuttoning or unzipping them. The seat was cold. She regretted, idly, the warm urine leaving her body. At the house Alastair will embrace Caroline and say, "Why do you always wear a belt?" and take the belt off, snaking it through the belt loops, holding its long tooth in his hand. In the restroom, before she washed her hands, she put her coat on the ledge of the sink; the sink had a motion sensor, and the tap went on automatically, staining the coat. The entire left sleeve was soaked. When she walked out of the restroom and through the brightly lit welcome center to the parking lot, she looked like she was wearing a drowned animal. The lights, like snow globes, illuminated the falling sharp-edged snowflakes, snow like stars, a Pleiades of snow. For a moment, in her drowned coat, Caroline could not find her keys, and as she fumbled with her handbag, two men appeared in the empty spot beside her. Could they help her? The men had been pleasant, if a little drunk, and meant no harm. Quince and Stout, a little pantomime. They thought she looked lost. They would be happy to buy her a drink. What happened when Caroline got back into the car?

A shrug is not an answer. And every circle of light cast by the parking-lot lanterns is not a sign of fairies at work, or a mirror made of rowan leaves. It is not made of rowan leaves, it

is circled by rowan leaves! Here is the little girl in her smocked
dress smelling the boxwood under the trellis. A girl who would
refuse to be a Brownie because she was afraid to look in the
mirror, and who grew up to be a witch. A witch? A girl who is
afraid. Are witches afraid? They are more afraid than anyone:
they need spells to keep them safe. And they know the power
of spells, which other people do not. Other people do not need
spells. That is what Pom told Caroline one morning, brushing
her teeth before school. You are telling this story about Caroline in the parking lot with the snow globes because that is the
kind of story you always tell: it is a story in which Caroline is
helpless in some way but charming; if another person told it, he
would not emphasize her charm but her incompetence, which
is irritating. Every story Caroline tells is about her clumsiness,
her very own way of being daft, her fecklessness. Caroline is all
these things! She is not. She is calculating and she is mercenary.
You knew that. It is the reason at bottom that everyone who
loves her sooner or later finds out that she is not safe. Because
Caroline is not safe.

On Sunday I wrote back to your letter of a week ago. Have
I answered? No. As I type, leaves fall into my coffee. The cold
weather is coming. You are wearing a hat. Yes, but not a fur
hat. The children are asleep upstairs. Where is Caroline? She
has stopped the car in the alley of oak trees after the covered
bridge. The trees are immense and covered with snow. Beyond
them the river is so slow it seems to sidle backward to where
it feeds into the lake, which is like a pair of spectacles: a figure
eight. When she gets out of the car she feels the air around her
eddy, she is suspended in the spirit level. When she returns
along this road, the long past without Alastair, a funnel which

has turned her out at this moment, will be the past and something else will have happened. What if it is the same thing?
Then she will know that. For a moment, the engine turns over
but nothing happens. Then it lurches. She thinks, sitting in the
car, listening to the motor clear its throat, that she is a woman
on a deserted road in the deep country beside a frozen river, on
her way to meet a man she has not seen in twenty-five years,
who is a madman.

When Caroline was small she would fall asleep in the back of
the car. The car was huge, black, an Oldsmobile sedan. The seats
were leather. She was in her pajamas, and when the car stopped
her father carried her up the flagstone stairs to the house. Each
step was one stone, the stairs were steep, and curved under the
rhododendron. The boxwood on the bank of the stairs were her
height when she stood next to them. The leaves fit on her fingers
like little caps. Even asleep she could smell the boxwood, like
leaves burning far off. When her children were small the eldest
would write notes from fairies for the other children to find at
the bottom of the pine woods. It was a house that belonged to
their grandparents. It was fall. In the summer Caroline rented
another house, on a bluff, with a leak in the ceiling. She did not
like staying in the same house as her father. When she was small
Caroline's father lifted her up out of the car and she put her
arms around his neck. If it was the weekend the top button of
his shirt would be open and she could smell the laundry smell
of his white undershirt. In the leather seams of the car seat sand
clotted along the stitches. Every summer they went to the beach.
And sometimes in the winter. When Caroline got out of the car
on the way to meet Alastair and looked at the frozen river, she
thought, *He is a madman and I am mad.*

Some more facts about Caroline and Alastair: *he liked to tie Caroline up.* How did he do it? It was hard to tie her to the bed because there was no headboard and she generally slipped out of the bonds that were loops of ties from Barneys and Brooks Brothers, not the real McCoy, hilarious, really. He did not tie them particularly tight, and she could release herself quickly. That they were not tied tight, and did not cut into her skin, was in one way the problem, because Alastair at once could not stand tying Caroline up and could not stand not to. Later, for these purposes, he sometimes brought girls to the apartment on Eighty-Fourth Street, but it was many years before Caroline knew that.

*

For many years after they parted she had had the same dream. She was buying a train ticket to see Alastair, but when she read the ticket issued by the dream, it was the wrong one, to another destination altogether; she knew this, although she could not read the blurry print. She discovered the mistake anew each time—what she learned in one dream dissolved and did not carry over to another; once again, she would need to change trains, and to wait in the station in the snow. From a public telephone booth at the end of the station platform, she would try to call him, and no one would pick up, although she could see the telephone ringing, a black telephone with its cord attached to the wall, or on the knotty pine chest of drawers upstairs, and she could see it ringing, too, when she tried the second number at the house in town, with the mural of the weeping willow on the wall. No one picked up, or sometimes she picked up; a shadow cast on the wall by the moonlight streaming through the fanlight over the door. She could see herself, in an old green jacket she had not worn for years, her shoulders hunched, answering the telephone in the cold and empty house. She knew both numbers by heart, *a memoria*. They are on her cell phone, even now, along with the numbers of the dead, which she cannot bear to erase, and even voice mails, in which they speak. You will remember the bridge, Alastair said. It was hard to see the bridge in the snow, and it was growing dark. Even though it was snowing and the car windows were closed, she could hear the tidal river under the ice beyond the trees. It moved like the tail of an enormous animal. The river was frozen in some places, and broken up in others, as if the tail had cracked the ice. Where the water was open it was black and cluttered with leaves and broken branches. A few weeks ago, in a letter to Caroline, five or six years after this November, Alastair described how his dog liked to swim in the river, and when it was time to leave, he used the command "Come now." *How are you?* the letter asked. Has she answered? No, not yet.

*

What she remembered was the sound of water. A great sluice over-head. The rocks were slick, but they could go behind the waterfall to a cave which had been scooped out of the brown rock by the rushing water. She was with her brothers. Inside the cave was a pool, lacy with spray from the cataract of the waterfall, a curtain of green. The sound was tremendous. It beat on her ears; her knees drummed the water. She was a puppet pulled by the pulley of water as it went over the cliff. The roar came down from far over her head. She could stand in the pool, the spools of water green and white and gold, phantasms. Once, she had seen inside a whale's mouth, the teeth translucent, and

now she was looking out; it was impossible to peer from the maw of
the cave through the spumes of water. Beside her, her brothers were
fish, butting her legs; they were smaller than she was, and the water
came up higher, but they were not afraid, whooping in the roar, holding her hands, their free hands like pinwheels inches from the spray.
They were in their bathing suits. It was hot outside but inside the
cave it was cool, almost cold. It was a place that had not been dry for
millennia, when the earth looked different than it did now, sandstone
and basalt, enormous slabs under a raging sun. Later when she held
the hands of her own children at the sea to keep them from being
knocked under, she remembered that sound in the cave, crouched like
a wave about to break over her head, as their hands pulled at her.

It was winter but it was summer where they were. For a few
years of her childhood there were holidays at the school break, palm
trees like grandees, muslin curtains, huge ceiling fans like helicopter
blades. After a while these stopped. She never knew why, or asked.
Then her parents went off by themselves in the taxi to the airport. Her
grandmother arrived and played solitaire. She misbehaved, she would
not come to the table; she ate sweets, secretly, in her room. The winter
of the waterfall she was nine or ten. In the rented house, there was a
copper bowl full of lemons in the middle of the table, mosquito nets
over the beds, floating from the ceiling like ghosts. Orange lizards ran
up and down the window frames, over the blue-tile floors, and the
yellow tile in the bathroom.

What was she doing at nine, in the bathroom with her father? She
is talking with her friend Helen in the kitchen in Wainscott—she is
grown up now, they have eight children between them, they are making
coronation chicken for fifteen people—the ceramic sugar bowl is the
exact same yellow, the color of an Easter egg. It was the summer she

was stung by the jellyfish, which left a handprint on her face that lasted for weeks, so that the other customers at the A&P turned away embarrassed. As a child, she had a brown birthmark in the shape of Australia on her shoulder that later disappeared. Now it was as if the sea she loved had summoned the mark from her skin: there it is; it was there all along. Helen is also an eldest child, something in the way she says "my father" opens the door of the house onto the beach in the place where it was summer, not winter. The patio floor was concrete, and the local boys split coconuts right there and gave her and her brothers, who were four and five, the flesh to eat for a quarter, the winter she said to her own father, under the roar of the shower, holding on to the white towel rack in the yellow bathroom, "I'm too old." She remembers the precise moment standing in the kitchen in Wainscott, in the old kitchen, before the hurricane when the tree crashed into the window—the cupboards began to open and close, spilling their contents, the miso and the maple syrup pooling on the sideboard. Like Caroline an eldest daughter. What does it mean if she said, I am too old? Her father larger, and she much smaller, the size of a cat going around the shrubbery, under the boxwood hedge beyond the trellis, into the hollow of webbed branches where she kept a button, a small shovel, a bar of chocolate nibbled by shrews, so that if you were to cut a cross section under the earth in which the boxwood stood, written in a wobbly, skewed hand that recently learned to form letters, written on a bookplate: This book belongs to Caroline. *On the bookplate was a drawing of a teetering pile of books. Her knuckles were white where she held the towel rack, as if she were resisting being dragged, or pulled. But her eyes were screwed tight.*

*

But that is how Caroline first appeared, yes? When? You had gone in the winter with the children to Captiva. You told me that in the bathroom there was a yellow-tile floor, and in the bedroom there was a white bureau, with yellow trim. You wrote me a description of the room, and you told me that you saw Caroline in the mirror. And you began then to think of Caroline in the ice and the snow. But not of her hands on the towel rack, that came later. No. Yes, that came later.

For Caroline there was one answer, for Alastair another. A yes, and a no. The lines of print wobble, the eddies around the letters rearrange themselves. But for Caroline the present and the future tense are imperfect. The word *stop* shut and opened doors. But when did it start? She told him, "Stop, I'm too old." There was never a time, not even in the continuous present, when she could speak about this to her father, her father who is now an old man, in his houndstooth jacket and mustache, his gout, his inability—still—to be interrupted. When she was a child he would come into her room and stroke her hair until she fell asleep, a man with whom she never once felt safe, with whom she went out every day in the summer into the harbor in a small boat, where she tacked again and again around a life preserver, thrown into the water, in order to learn how to save someone who had fallen overboard from drowning. Anything can happen.

When Caroline left her second husband, forty years later, her father came to the house where she was staying with her children and demanded that her daughters leave with him. Her eldest daughter was sixteen. No, she said, and yanked her arm from where he had touched her. Later she would say, I did it for you, Mama, don't say I never did anything for you, smoke coming out of her mouth as she took a drag of her cigarette

in the garden. But she did not want to go with her grandfather. Don't smoke near the window, please. From the back,
my mother looks fourteen. My mother is a child, my parents
are so original. And, she said to him, you are not to talk to me
about my mother ever again. On that same trip, the winter
she was nine years old, Caroline was taken by her father to an
aluminum mine, in which he had an interest, and was given a
cold glass of lemonade, under an umbrella. At the falls, putting
her hand through the curtain of water, she could not see her
hand in front of her face. Even now, the word *aluminum* catches
in her mouth, unpronounceable. Do you see that tin can? It
doesn't see you. The aluminum in the mine glinting. In Maine
it is snowing so hard the flakes—it snows hard. It is only when
she can say no that she can say yes.

What did Caroline learn, her fist clenched to the white ceramic towel rack, in the rented house, near ——. It was 1968.
I am trying to picture Caroline at eight or ten, in her one-piece
Speedo bathing suit. Or in her nightgown? What time was it?
Where was her mother? That is the story, isn't it? Or part of it,
another story for another time. Last night Caroline was up most
of the night coughing, the catch in her throat throttling her.
There was no one to call to say how sick she was. She has made
her bed, and she is lying in it. Does she want to be alone? Is it
because she knows she needs to end this, to get out of it some-
how? Did that happen? No, I don't think so, *ma chi sa*? If she did
not want to be alone, she would not be in love with you! I am
not being clear, I do not want to get into it. We can talk about
it later: it's not the worst thing that happened to her. What is
the worst thing? *You push too hard. Every damn minute.* Not to be
unloved but to be the nexus of violence. To not be able *to tell*

the difference. To not be happy to tell. In the mirror in the small bathroom with the yellow tiles a man picked up his hand and struck a child repeatedly, enraged. It was 1968. Alastair was eleven. Caroline was nine. I think that is right. I am trying to picture Caroline at nine, in her one-piece Speedo bathing suit. Or in her nightgown? What time was it? She was, it is true, an impossible child, a child given to tantrums, to hurt feelings, a child who grew up unable to bear it when her parents entered a room, who could not embrace her parents, which angered them. But she cannot. She knows the place where the wolf lies down. Caroline, girded against the snow, in her hat and coat, waiting for a phantom to call, a man who later that year, that summer, next winter, will embrace her at the house where Nick has come to meet Mimi, to convince her to give herself up, as if it mattered who had pulled the trigger, to save his daughters, one of whose is Mimi's and one of whose mother is someone else. A minor, forgettable film. Caroline goes to the movies in order to make sense of her dreams, like anyone else. Alastair could never harm Caroline, and that was why from the very start it was finished. But that did not mean she could not be harmed.

*

Alastair had said in his note that he would get there early to open up the house, but when she arrived, finally, down the alley of pine trees, the stone wall almost covered with snow, there was no one there. Her boots were inadequate. She had not thought of it. She went up to the house but the door was shut with a padlock. It was extremely cold. It occurred to Caroline that this was folly. She tested the idea of being afraid, prodding it, as if she were testing lightly to see if someone was awake. She knew, from when she would come here with Alastair in the winter, that the snow which was now falling lightly could in a moment be impassable, she would not be able to see her hand in front of her face. Caroline thought, fleetingly, that perhaps the best thing she could see in front of her face was her own hand; she was in the wood in the dark in a dream, waiting for Alastair, whom she knew too much about and whom she had not seen in almost thirty years. Later he would write, first that summer and then years later, Do you know the latch is still broken from where I tore it off the hinges that afternoon? When his mother saw the broken lock in the spring she said, Of course, someone has broken in. He did not enlighten her. Instead, he said: There's no point in fixing it. If someone wants to break in, they can break in: there's nothing to take.

There was everything to take. Caroline waited for fifteen minutes in the snow. After a little time had passed, she was simply waiting to see what would happen. It was entirely possible he would not come. If he did not come, she would be in a different story than the one she had imagined, but it was possible, she knew, to imagine anything. She knew that then? Yes. That is terrible. She learned that early, yes? She learned that if something else happens, it is simply a different story, and that stories, too, can be told differently. The story of Oedipus is different if we think: Laius and Jocasta were very young, they could have decided differently. Caroline learned early that anything could happen, that the lash could come, and because of this she learned to be indifferent to whether or not it came, because the way to protect herself was not to care which it

would be. I think Oedipus would have married Jocasta in the
end. No matter what? Yes.

*

Caroline is standing in the crystallizing snow waiting for
Alastair. She is not waiting for the phone to ring. She is hatless,
in the cold. Later she will have a fur hat and fur boots, but not
now. It is quiet, where she is waiting, by the locked door. The
casement windows have a skin of ice that puckers at the frame.
The slate step to the door is drifted over with snow. Nearby
the tracks of an animal, a fox, a deer, have drawn a lopsided circle in the snow—she knows nothing at all about animal tracks,
although years ago Alastair tried to teach her, and bought her
a book with tiny footprints which he put in her stocking at
Christmas. The language of the woods evades her. She is folded
in time, standing in the snow, infinite, between again and ago.
It cannot end, the conflict between Caroline and Caroline,
Caroline and Alastair, Alastair and Alastair.

But I invented Caroline, and I want it to end. Yes, you invented her but she is not yours—you knew who she was because you recognized her when I described her to you: *una
ragazza nella neve*. That's true, but now I am writing this to take
her back. She will take her hat and coat and slip out the door;
she will not wait for you in a doorway, looking up at your window. You are writing it so that many things might be possible;
you are trying to wake yourself up from a dream. Are Caroline
and Alastair the point? No, it is the moment when Caroline
wakes from a trance. A trance of what? Children, and school,

and standing at the stove. Aurora, too, wakes from sleep. Yes, and we do not know anything about how that turned out, really, do we?

Caroline is waiting in the snow, between the future and the past, waiting for Alastair. He does come, doesn't he? Yes. He is driving a gray-green Subaru station wagon, with snow tires. He has become a man who drives a car with snow tires. He lives in Maine. Caroline does not have snow tires. The car chugs over the little rise and then skates down like a bird to meet Caroline's car where she has parked it by the pond.

Caroline is waiting in the snow in her fur hat and boots, waiting for Alastair to call. Her cell phone is inside her glove. She is a stone's throw from where thirty years ago Alastair tried to hack a burrow for himself under the frozen locusts. Caroline is waiting in the snow for Alastair to appear, in November, a few months earlier. He arrives driving a car with snow tires, full of groceries. He has not stopped trying to feed Caroline. It is as if no time has passed. He has brought chocolate and cheese and crackers and a bottle of Lagavulin. And coffee and milk. A box of pasta. Sausages. When he gets out of the car, he is wearing a fleece pullover. He looks exactly the same, but thicker. Behind his glasses his eyes are the color of agates; this has not changed. The lines around his eyes look like the bird feet he tried to teach her to read when they were children. She takes one step toward him in her inadequate boots. When he has her in his arms he reaches around and cups her elbows in his hands. It is an instantly recognizable gesture, Alastair pulling at the joints of her elbows, and Caroline starts to cry. She is too deep in the story to know that it is a story, and that it has a beginning, a middle, and an end. They do not know it yet, which is one reason they are ridiculous, standing in the snow, Caroline's mouth on Alastair's jacket, like a horse nuzzling for sweets.

Caroline is standing in the snow with a man she has loved for many years whose preoccupation now is watching women who like to hurt themselves. She is part of this. She has—in a way—what is the new word: *enabled* this. This is what she thinks? And for Caroline, Alastair is the story which is not the story, the story which is inside the Japanese fan, which rarely opens, only now, when it is cold and still. Here is the house, and here is the steeple, the pine tree, its pen-and-ink shadow brushing the house. The calligraphy is too small to read.

ELLIE ANDREWS: By the way, what's your name?
PETER WARNE: What's that?
ELLIE ANDREWS: Who are you?
PETER WARNE: Who me? (*smiling*) I'm the whippoorwill that cries in the night. I'm the soft morning breeze that caresses your lovely face.

He could not see them, that is: he could see them on the screen but he could not touch them. It was different than it had been with Mona in the house of wattles, the white laundry in the humid air, never drying, sucking on *jalaato* in Mogadishu, blocks from the starry Shebelle River, the city where Caroline would not go, where she refused to go, where he had burrowed into the heat like a vole under the sediment of his own history, nicking at the roots, thinking then, *Anything can happen.* He sat up late at night with the dog in the room over the garage and watched the girls on the screen. Sometimes he found one girl, and kept her for a while. There was one called Ruby. She was a singer, she sang sometimes at a dive bar in Portland called Stewie's, where he went to watch her. She lived not far away, and I think he met her once or twice in a hotel or motel, but when she was there it was difficult for him to touch her so they went back to the screen. He would not touch them? How did it work? The girls did what he told them to do. Yes. That was it. Did he describe this to Caroline? Yes. She was complicit in this? It was complicated between Caroline and Alastair. Yes, you think so. *Quest' è quello che pensi.* It was never boys? No. But Alastair saw himself in the mirror. It was the same mirror as the mirror over the chipped sink, where he stood washing his hands, the sleeves of his Oxford shirt rolled up over his forearms. Caroline did not see herself? No, she turned away. You see that sardine can? I looked in the mirror and saw— *No, Caroline would not do that.* What was Caddy Compson doing in the pear tree? Caroline was nine. What was she doing? Telling stories. That part is hard to tease out. When she was a child she had a friend whose mother would send them on treasure hunts in the woods. You followed a string looped from tree to tree, there were small prizes along the way, a puppet, a tin car tied to the string, but the last prize was always a cake in a big box, and whoever found it first would have the first piece and dole out pieces of cake to the others. But the woods were filled with brambles, and by the time the children reached the cake they would be scraped and bleeding. There was a moment when Caroline said no and Alastair said yes, but in some ways the reverse is true. She said yes and he said no; she said yes to not knowing what happened, and he said no, this has happened.

But she said no to the smile song? Yes, she said no to the smile song, carried down the capillaries of rivers.

*

She flinches when her father touches her as she has always flinched, and he continues to make her do this, to make her feel that it is her fault that she flinches. She is afraid of small spaces, of places underground, of not being able to leave, so she leaves first, or she makes it impossible to stay. She makes herself the opportunity for someone else to behave badly; in the end, it is her fault. After a visit to her parents with her children, Caroline, in the car, flips down the mirror on the passenger side and checks her reflection. She thinks, *Brownie points*. When she was a child her father wore ties printed with little badges. Years ago, when Louie was small, she said, "I always know when we are almost there because you check your lipstick in the mirror," and Caroline was delighted at having become a woman who checked her lipstick in the mirror predictably. The same daughter who said, "You always think it is going to rain, because you always have your sunglasses on." As you can see, yawning now, bored to tears, wishing you could disappear and that Caroline would just stop it—and you could disappear, you have disappeared, you are no stranger to disappearance. But now Caroline is having trouble leaving the yellow-tiled bathroom, where Alastair has the cold tap running. Can the wrong way be the right start? One foot in front of the other: the sound of bells, ice cracking, water jangling in the basin, blood beating in Alastair's temples, a bowl full of lemons, a tiny boat made of paper, tipped.

Caroline is standing in the snow, in her snow globe. When her children were small she read them the story of the Snow Queen, a tale in which the ending takes a long time to happen, as if it were a story unfolding inside a story, an origami snow-flake that holds another snowflake, until it retreats into a shard of salt. It is unwise to turn and look back, we know that. When in the story Kai disappears, Gerda sets out to find him and meets with misadventure. Time after time she is miraculously saved. Here is a little bit of it, near the end:

"I can give her no greater power than she has already," said the woman; "don't you see how strong that is? How men and animals are obliged to serve her, and how well she has got through the world, barefooted as she is. She cannot re-ceive any power from me greater than she now has, which consists in her own purity and innocence of heart. If she cannot herself obtain access to the Snow Queen, and re-move the glass fragments from little Kai, we can do nothing to help her."

Gerda, it is true, says the Lord's Prayer, in order to pass through the gates of the Snow Queen's palace. When she passes through the gate, after she has walked some way, she finds Kai in the middle of a frozen lake, rigid with cold. He is the boy inside the mirror, the perimeter rimmed by the rowan's terrible leaves. The lake is called the Mirror of Reason. Does that mean that everything reflected in the lake is backward, a serpent under the water biting his tail? *Chi lo sa?* He has fallen under the spell of the Snow Queen, and he has been given a task: he must spell out the word *eternity* with pieces of ice, which lie scattered around him like pieces of a Chinese puzzle.

It is so cold that Kai has no language, the pieces of ice break in his fingers, which have so little warmth in them that the ice he touches does not melt. But when Gerda sees him she knows nothing of this—she runs up to him and kisses him, weeping; her tears melt the splinter in his heart and dislodge the shard in his eye, and he is happy again; even the shards of ice are happy, and dance on the frozen mirror of their own accord, spelling out the word *eternity* so that the Snow Queen must free Kai, according to her word, and they return rosy and glad to the village, which is suddenly not far away, to the window boxes and the roses, which bloom hot and humid, and the grandmother who quotes from scripture. "Verily I say unto you, Except ye be converted, and become as little children, ye shall not enter into the kingdom of heaven."

The story has always vexed Caroline. Why would the Snow Queen keep her word? And why would she give Kai a task that would free him if he completed it? Was it because she felt sure he could not complete it and wanted to torment him? Why the word *eternity*? Wasn't Kai destined to spend eternity in his Chinese puzzle of ice shards? But was Kai, under the spell of the jangling bells, eager to be freed? Was Kai's trance—brought on by himself, by giving in to the Snow Queen's enchantment—his choice? He had a shard of the mirror in his eye, didn't he? From whose point of view is the story told, Kai's or Gerda's? Gerda is searching for Kai, the search is the story she tells herself about her life, but is Kai waiting for Gerda to find him? Does he think he is lost? The arc of the story demands resolution or even redemption, that Caroline plum, but in her favorite story, "The Little Mermaid," written by the same madman in Copenhagen with a tallow candle that spewed soot—for these stories are *made up* by a boy who was tormented at school, son of a washerwoman, who grew to a question mark—the mermaid in her sorrow, her feet pierced by swords, voiceless, dissolves into foam in the waves: a story about the price of desire. It is a truer story, she thinks, than a story in which tears melt a shard of ice. Caroline, who cleaves to Alastair's story even as she turns the pages of the book, is standing in the snow, riven with longing, as if by an iron stake through her heart. Even in the snow a few figures lope around the reservoir.

*

But what was Caroline waiting for, in the park, in her fur hat and boots, years ago? She was waiting for Alastair to call. Did he call? Yes. He called on and off, for months. They spent a few days in Mexico, she met him a number of times in Maine, he came to New York. He was in love with someone else, a student, by then. He left his wife, then went back. Caroline went to see him, in a horrible flat above a shop, on the main street of the town. And then when that was over, he was in love with Caroline again. *I have never stopped loving you*, he wrote, just a few weeks ago. Soon it will be snowing where he is, the screen a blue pool, the dog sleeping on the hearthrug. Outside the window the snow will be coming down, lightly at first, thrown salt, for luck, then harder and faster, a disco ball of snow, until he cannot see the hand in front of his face. He does not want to see the hand in front of his face, the hand that then began to wash the cuts on his arm with such tenderness.

In real time—that is, a few weeks ago—in New York, Caroline received an email from Alastair in response to one she had written the night before. The beginning of hers read, *And now it is me who has taken a long time to reply, but between us, does it matter?* He wrote, *I want to say to your first sentences that this is just our very slow and careful game of ping-pong, maybe the kind played with zero gravity like a game on Mars . . . And I guess we would know if the message said,* "Come, now," *which is what I say to the dog when he swims in Sheep River. You are not drowning, are you?* Caroline thinks it over, like someone picking herself up after a fall. No, she is not drowning.

You have told me this before. But they are still speaking to each other, Caroline and Alastair? Yes, they are. Shall I tell you about it? Yes. They are not exactly speaking to each other, but in some other way they do not ever stop speaking to each other. Years later, after a plague had descended, and it was impossible to see almost anyone at all, she watched a video in which an old and famous dancer directed four dancers in a story she loved, about a goblin and a princess. Each dancer was in his own room, in Moscow, in Santa Barbara, in New York, in Belgrade, but they communicated with each other by directing their dancing toward the other rooms, which were invisible to them, and by the connections they made, pulling each other to each other, and pushing away. That is how it is, between them. But it is not, exactly, like speaking to you. Tell me. Can I do it quickly, in a kind of shorthand? Yes, because I want to get on with it and get to the next part. You are nodding your head; does that mean yes? That is what it usually means. Because I am a little bored with it. Yes.

*

The last time Caroline saw Alastair was in July 1985, on Central Park West on the corner of Seventy-Second Street, on the park side; that is, the last time she saw him before, years later, she saw him again. Twenty-five years later, she is in a hotel room in Minneapolis, where she has gone with a friend, a patron of the arts, to see an actor in a play at the Guthrie Theater. Outside it is snowing. One wall of the hotel room is windowed, and the opposite wall, above a long, low bureau, is mirrored. She has opened the curtains, and so it is snowing on both sides of the room, outside, and in the mirror. She is thinking about Lara in *Doctor Zhivago.* She owns a fur hat almost exactly like the hat worn by Julie Christie, on her long, cold drive in the snow, but she has forgotten to bring it with her. The hat was given to her by a great-aunt, who said, "I don't wear this but you will." Caroline is the kind of person who is often given things that other people thought they wanted or would wear but have put aside. Another way of saying this is that she keeps things long after someone else might have given them up. There was a detour to get to the hotel because the voice of the GPS, a woman with an Australian accent, directed the driver, her friend, a philanthropist who owned aluminum mines in which the workers were treated ruthlessly, and who almost always insisted on driving himself, to a trailer park rather than to the hotel in Minneapolis. He had put in the wrong address. On the drive, it had already begun snowing. There were four people in the car: Caroline, her friend, his wife, and an Italian woman who her friend hoped would be on the board of a theater company— a board on which he served as chairman. This woman, whose name was Paola, was not enamored of the snow, or of the little visit, after an hour of driving around, to the trailer park, and she had given up talking to Caroline, who was staring out the window and who had adopted the air of someone in a trance. Instead she was speaking at length about the problem of getting someone to fix the drains in a house she owned near Pienza. Instead of drains Caroline was thinking idly, as if she were drawing with a ballpoint pen on the margins of a page of math problems, of a play she had seen many years ago, in which a child is buried in a backyard very much like the yards around the houses in the trailer park. At the end of the play a man called Tilden comes out onstage carrying the mummified remains of the child. The friend with whom she had gone to see the play—they were both undergraduates—now lived in Italy, but in Viterbo, nowhere near Pienza.

Outside the hotel room at the Excelsior in Minneapolis, it is snowing. Caroline is getting dressed to meet her friend and his wife to go to the theater to see *Peer Gynt*. She has brushed her hair, but that is as far as she has gotten in the complicated project of dressing herself. She has taken a shower and she is wearing a white terry-cloth hotel bathrobe. If she wants to take the robe home, the hotel will add eighty-five dollars to her bill. Instead of getting dressed, she is considering this. She is five years younger than she is now. She is wondering when and if she will pick up the telephone and call Alastair, who lives in Maine, where it is also snowing, who is quietly having what used to be called a nervous breakdown, who—she knows—is alone this weekend with his younger daughter, because his wife has taken his elder daughter to a cross-country ski meet. They are a family very involved in ski meets, and race times, and driving children around in the snow with gear in the back of the car. Often, he calls her from the parking lot where he is sitting in the car with the motor running and the heat on. He drinks in the car. He is the kind of man who keeps a bottle of whisky in his office, under an old sweatshirt in his desk drawer. When Caroline looks in the mirror, it is snowing; she is a woman in a white terry-cloth robe in the snow. Outside the hotel, snow frosts the leaves of the rowan branches.

In the hotel in Minneapolis where Caroline is getting dressed, it is snowing in the mirror. She is deciding whether or not to pick up the telephone and place a call. Because she does not want the call to appear on her cell phone record, she will make the call through the hotel switchboard, and pay for it separately with cash, and then pay the rest of her bill with a credit card. These kinds of thoughts both exhaust Caroline and exhilarate her, as if she were playing a game in which she is making up the rules as she goes along. That is what she thinks. As usual she is wrong. Looking in the mirror Caroline puts on a pair of fawn velvet trousers, a red-and-pink-striped shirt made of flannel which fastens with gigantic jeweled buttons. The shirt, which is beautiful, once belonged to the mother of one of her daughter's boyfriends—a woman who is also the goddaughter of a close friend's mother. This woman gave it to Louie and she gave it to Caroline. Over the shirt she puts on a houndstooth jacket which once belonged to the same great-aunt who gave Caroline her fur hat. She looks in the mirror where it is snowing and piles her hair on top of her head and fastens it with long pins. At that time Caroline usually piled her hair on top of her head. Everywhere she went, she left pins. She is wondering if she will pick up the phone and call. About now, he is most likely making dinner. She has never been to the house where he is living this winter, so she cannot picture the kitchen exactly, so instead she pictures a kitchen in his mother's house, a few days before Christmas twenty-five years ago.

Strangely, she cannot remember anything at all about the
outside of Alastair's parents' house in Maine, or the entrance,
or the lawn in front and behind, although she is sure there was
a lawn; it was a low nineteenth-century clapboard house, with
oddly placed additions, a greenhouse, a gun room that smelled
of dog. In the dining room—which she does remember, where
she sat for a few strained dinners—although they had lived
together for two years, Caroline was still a new girlfriend, and
they had liked the one before better, a tall, dark-haired girl with
a self-deprecating air that she would retain into middle age—
there was a mural of a weeping willow, a village scene dotted
with flowers. There was an octagonal bench around the base
of the willow. The mural replicated the village green outside
the window, but now the house and the green were covered
in snow. Frost covered the kitchen windows, and someone
had drawn, with a fingernail, a picture of a house with smoke
coming out of the chimney on the windowpane, in the frost.
The village was called Odense. The artist had painted a green
river winding in back of the willow tree. The house drawn in
the frost matched the house in the mural, the same four-up
and four-down windows, the exact same curl of smoke. In the
kitchen, Caroline began to think about how interesting it was
to look out through the windowpane of a house that had been
drawn, probably by Alastair's younger sister, who was called
Whip, in the frost on the windowpane. Whip was twelve and
looked like an angel who had touched down but would not
be staying long. Alastair, who even by then figured in Caroline's story like a giant moth whose wings alternately shelter
and frighten her with their ceaseless beating, liked to take pictures of Whip when she was sleeping. He also liked taking

pictures of Caroline. He liked being alone in the dark as im-
ages floated up from the acid bath like dreams. He particularly
liked taking pictures in strange or abandoned places, under
bridges and aqueducts and strange pockets where litter piled
up. He had grown up in the city unhindered by supervision
and knew all the places where a fifteen-year-old could get high
without anyone noticing, and he liked to take Caroline to these
places and take photographs. Last summer, he had taken a series of pictures of a shipwreck near a house that belonged to
Caroline's parents that was slowly rotting away. The kitchen
was warm. It was nine o'clock in the morning. In the warm
kitchen Alastair's grandmother, in a black dress with an old
blue ski jacket that Caroline recognized as having belonged
to Whip, was making tomato sauce. Last night, when they'd
arrived, the night before Christmas Eve, she was already at the
stove, with her black dress and shawl. Even in the kitchen, she
held tight to her handbag, a cavernous affair of cracked black
leather, as though she suspected that if she left it unattended
it would disappear. This was not entirely unfounded; Alastair's
brother, Otto, did not then believe in ownership. In Odense,
Caroline kept cash inside an old copy of *Hangman's Holiday*
tucked into the bookcase in Alastair's childhood bedroom,
with a paper clip on the binding. Otto did not touch Whip's
things. She mentioned this once to Alastair. He does not want
anything she has, he said, which translated into: Whip has no
money. In the three days in the house, during which it was
snowing so hard that it was not possible to think of going out,
Caroline conceived a deep and unswerving fear of Alastair's
grandmother, who pinched her arm, like a witch in a fairy tale.
Her name was Angelina Alighieri.

At nine in the morning Angelina was making tomato sauce
and Caroline, on the other side of the kitchen, was waiting
for the water to move through the coffee filter. It was moving
slowly. She was at the beginning of years in which the time she
spent waiting for coffee would multiply, until there were elastic
bands of hours in which, half-awake, she waited for the sound
of an espresso machine, or the saturation of a French press, or
later, when she was lazy, the beep of a German drip machine indicating water had passed through the grounds. On the counter
Angelina had put four large cans of peeled tomatoes, each with
a label that showed a smiling, black-haired girl carrying a tray
on her head packed with tomatoes. She was set like a jewel in
a wreath of green leaves that looked nothing like the leaves of
tomato vines. Gravity was not doing its usual work on the tray
of tomatoes, which was tilted over the girl's head like the wing
of a circling biplane. The girl wore a peasant blouse and a very
white apron which was miraculously not stained with tomato
juice. The label was in Italian. *Pomodori Pelati San Marzano.* The
brand was Nina. You must only buy peeled tomatoes, and you
must only buy San Marzano, said Angelina. It was 1983. Angelina had conjured up these cans from—where? Nowhere. It was
imaginary tomato sauce cooked in an imaginary house in the
snow, with a picture of a weeping willow in springtime painted
two hundred years ago on the dining room wall, and a picture
of a house with a smoking chimney etched with a fingernail
into a windowpane coated with frost.

Certain things stick in Caroline's head. *Buy San Marzano
tomatoes.* Do not cut the stems of flowers the same length before
you put them in a vase. If you see a run in your stocking when

you are leaving the house, pretend it happened when you were
getting out of the taxi. Do not wear white shoes after Labor
Day. They called me the Hyacinth Girl. Last night—thirty years
later—she received a letter from Alastair. *I'd love to meet* [insert
name of Caroline's youngest daughter here, an odd name, one
she could not have predicted] *. . . would love in some way to . . .
I don't know . . . be past the Sturm und Drang, and yet sometimes I
think the Sturm und Drang is all that keeps me going.* Caroline is
aware that this is true. The day before she arrived in Minneapolis, she had gone to see Anna Magnani in *Rome, Open City*, and
sat in the third row in the almost empty theater, *Credi che non
mi vergogni di essere sposata nelle mie condizioni?* Don't you think
I'm ashamed to be married in my condition? Magnani's small
mustache looks as if it is made of tiny metal filings, which could
be drawn by a magnet on a face made with a marker on a sheet
of cellophane. In the theater, Caroline closed her eyes. Lately,
she has gone to the movies two or three times a week, usually
by herself, and she has seen two films in which a door is opened
by a magnet on the opposite side of the door. She is the kind of
person who, despite evidence to the contrary, looks for portents
and spells, sticks in the forest, magic. She said on the telephone
last night, to a friend who is interested in birdcalls, who has
described to her in some detail the sound of a kingfisher's cry,
"I am being pulled apart by wild animals."

One evening in Minneapolis in a snowstorm five years ago,
Caroline tries to imagine a kitchen where Alastair, who has
been drinking all afternoon, is making tomato sauce for his
youngest daughter. She has trouble imagining Alastair in any
situation in which she is not present, and so she imagines the
kitchen in Odense. They have not seen each other for a long

time, except for about nine hours, total, in the last few months. She did not see him at all for twenty-three years, which is exactly half her life, counted in days and hours. As he is a few years older than she is, the percentage of time he has not seen her is slightly less, and Caroline feels that this represents some essential truth about the two of them: she has taken up slightly less space. When she does see Alastair, she thinks about him more often; when Alastair does not see her, the opposite is true: he thinks of her all the time. She knows this because he has told her. "I don't need to think of you," says Jerry, in a play Caroline and Alastair saw together in New York, twenty-five years ago. Many years later when she took her godson to see a revival of this play, about the telescopic nature of adultery, in London—he was twenty-two, only a year or two older than Caroline had been when she first saw it—he came out of the theater into the alley of Earlham Street and said, "*Nobody* behaves that way," and Caroline thought to herself, *Even I was never that young.* At twenty-two, she already knew about betrayal; like Otto, she is not good at knowing what belongs to other people. But what is a revival? she thought. When she was a girl, she was often taken to the theater by her grandmother, who would sigh and say how much better the production had been when it first opened. What she understands now is that what was better was newness, and the distant evening itself, her grandmother young in a new dress, her grandfather's hair still red. She cannot decide herself if the first time she saw the play it was better, now that she has seen it three, even four, times. The play, which moves backward in time rather than forward, is mixed up with the years she lived with Alastair, which seem like a rusty piece of chain just above the sand when the tide is out, an old line that keeps the dinghy tethered, where they sit, bundled against the wind, anchored in the freezing cold water. There had been no limits to the ways in which they made each other unhappy. Caroline has had many thoughts about this, none of them useful. One of the ways she drove Alastair crazy, for example, was by making him happy. Little instances of happiness. Even then, there was little she could find in herself to do about this. Now, five years or even six after the snowy day in Minneapolis, she knows that Alastair thinks about her all the time. She knows this because every so often he writes and tells her. It has not occurred to her that any commerce with Alastair, now, is a revival of their own private passion play.

I'm still learning how to keep some sort of day-to-day equilibrium. But I do really miss you. I've been having these dreams where I wake up inside my dream—I had this long, extended dream about marrying you—you were in a white dress by the pond and I was basically just putting my foot down and saying that I loved you and damn it, this was what I was going to do. I must have been about 25. I woke in tears.

Dressed in her hunting outfit, in the hotel in Minneapolis, before she went out for supper with the actor and his patron and the woman from Pienza who cared about drains, Caroline thought about calling Alastair, who was making dinner for his daughter in a kitchen whose windows were brushed by pine trees, five miles from the house where the painted willow covered the dining room wall and his grandmother clutched Caroline's wrist in her claw and told her to buy only San Marzano tomatoes. No seer, she had no idea that she would spend two decades of her life making tomato sauce, and that every time she opened a can of tomatoes she would feel that clutch around her wrist.

She did, or did not, call Alastair. It was immaterial, really. She did or did not know, then, that her husband, who paid the phone bill, was monitoring her calls. She was then too entranced to imagine that the cocoon of her marriage, in which, she thought, there was largesse and wry understanding, could hold only until the moment when a luna moth, flexing its wings, would sear itself on a flame. She did not understand that with a tap on the deep blue pool of the screen, she had lashed herself with a runner of brambles to the Snow Queen's sleigh. There were white flowers on the table when she arrived in the snow at her hotel. Her husband had sent them. In the mirror, snow was falling. She straightened her spine and put on her coat and went out of the room.

Is that it? The story? A woman who does or does not make a phone call? You can tell it, or not tell it. I am thinking that even now Caroline can conjure up Alastair's voice. It barely matters what he is saying, or what she says to him. Do you remember when we sat on the bench in the park and you said you were listening only to the sound of my voice? And I said you do not listen.

⚸

By the time Caroline met Alastair there were many songs on the airwaves about talking on the telephone. "Hanging on the Telephone," written by Jack Lee for his California band, the Nerves, was the first track on Blondie's 1978 LP, *Parallel Lines*. About the song Lee said, "Even people who hated me—and there were plenty—had to admit it was pretty great." Debbie Harry, the lead singer of Blondie, first heard it in the back of a cab in Tokyo. By the time she returned to the States, the Nerves had broken up and Blondie recorded the song, which opens with the sound of a ringing telephone. *I'm in the phone booth, it's the one across the hall / If you don't answer, I'll just ring it off the wall.* When asked if the ringing phone was a gimmick, the producer said, "A gimmick? This is Blondie." In 1962, on the flip side of the single "Two Lovers," Mary Wells, her voice made of gravel and cigarettes, sang Smokey Robinson's song "Operator":

> *I can hear my long-gone lover*
> *I've waited such a long, long time*
> *So please, operator,*
> *Put him on the line, I want him on the line*

On the Beatles' fourth British studio album, *Beatles for Sale*, released at the end of 1964, "No Reply" is the first track on the first side. John Lennon recalled, "I remember Dick James coming up to me after we did this one and saying, 'You're getting better now—that was a complete story.' Apparently, before that, he thought my songs wandered off."

> *I tried to telephone*
> *They said you were not home*
> *That's a lie*

In 1972, T. Rex released "Metal Guru." (In 2008 the e-zine *Freaky Trigger* would rate the song among the one hundred best rock-and-roll songs of all time.) The leader of the band, Marc Bolan, said about the lyrics *Metal guru, is it true? / All alone without a telephone*: "I believe in a God, but I have no religion. With

'Metal Guru', it's like someone special, it must be a Godhead. I thought how God would be, he'd be all alone without a telephone. I don't answer the phone any more."

The songs rippled out from the center of a black pond, the LP circling the turntable, the needle circling the grooves. Sometimes the needle skipped. The disc could so easily be scratched, and then the needle skipped some more, the arc it made was the arc of a skipping stone. Some records were listened to so often that there was a little hiss when the needle landed on the first pressed groove. It was an era of needles: the needle at the end of the phonograph arm, the needle and the damage done, panic in Needle Park, which was a few blocks in from the block on Central Park West where Caroline last saw Alastair in 1986, two stops on the IRT from the Eighty-Sixth Street stop, where for ten years she waited on the platform for the downtown train, minutes and hours she remembers as always freezing cold, though they could not have been. Because there was only one way to reach someone, except for a letter, which could take days, or weeks, if they were in Mozambique or London; if someone chose to let the telephone ring, it rang endlessly, the sound waves billowing out like nets or long lassos. In 1977, the Electric Light Orchestra's song "Telephone Line" was one of the top ten songs in the United States, Australia, and Britain, and number one in Canada.

> *Hello, how are you?*
> *Have you been all right*
> *Through all those lonely, lonely, lonely, lonely, lonely nights?*
> *That's what I'd say, I'd tell you everything*
> *If you'd pick up that telephone*

Like "Hanging on the Telephone," it starts with a ringing telephone. The guitarist Jeff Lynne, who wrote "Telephone Line," said, "To get the sound on the beginning, you know, the American telephone sound, we phoned from England to America to a number that we knew nobody would be at, to just listen to it for a while. On the Moog, we recreated the sound exactly by tuning the oscillators to the same notes as the ringing of the phone." Around the same time, the Modern Lovers recorded the song "I'm Straight," which Jonathan Richman described as capturing when "there's a moment on the phone where you get nervous and your heart starts to get a little sick and you get very sad."

I called this number three times already today
But I, I got scared, I put it
Back in place, I put my phone back in place.
I still don't know if I
Should have called up
Look, just tell me why don't ya if I'm out of place

A little sick and very sad, a lasso of sound, a telephone ringing in an empty room, held her as tightly as Kai was bound to the Snow Queen's sled, Gerda to the wire of love that drew her deeper into the forest where glittering fangs of ice hung like teeth from the trees, and the moon was full. In 1974, Joan Baez wrote "Diamonds and Rust," the title song on the album she released the next year. "You gonna sing that song," Dylan asked her, before the Rolling Thunder Revue tour, "about blue eyes and diamonds?" "The one I wrote for my husband?" she asked. "What the fuck do I know," he said. "Yeah," she said, "I'll sing it, if you like." Later to an interviewer she recounted how Dylan had called her and read her all the lyrics to "Lily, Rosemary, and the Jack of Hearts" from a phone booth somewhere in the Midwest. *It's just that the moon is full, and you happened to call.*

*

Like that, in her hotel room in the Midwest, Caroline did not need to speak to Alastair. In Minneapolis, it was so cold that there were enclosed corridors above the street, between the tall buildings. It wasn't necessary to go outside in order to travel across the city. Instead, you walked in glass arteries over the streets, which were sheathed in snow, where the red and green traffic signals flickered like hospital monitors. In the story of the Snow Queen, Gerda searches for Kai, and no one can help her. In the play, Solveig waits for Peer Gynt, who does or does not die in her arms. Where has Peer Gynt been since we last met? "Where was I as the one I should have been, whole and true, with the mark of God on my brow?"

Many of Alastair's conversations with Caroline are about the seasons: winter, spring, and summer. Because he could not speak to Caroline, because he felt—rightly or wrongly, or, better, falsely, there is that—that he had made a choice, or she had made one, which had taken him away from what he should have been; for Alastair, speaking to Caroline was to teeter on the brink of the known world. So, he wrote her letters late at night.

I'll miss that scene, if you don't mind. Caroline mulls this over. What scene would she like to miss? When the phone on her lap buzzes in the movie theater, she turns it off and waits for the voice mail message to appear. Then she leaves her shopping in the aisle—she had bought fruit at the market before the movie—and goes into the ladies' room in the lobby. The theater has four screening rooms. She buys a cup of Earl Grey tea from the kiosk, which also sells sandwiches: ham, smoked salmon, egg salad. Once in a while, she buys a chocolate bar. As a child, she read many stories in which a small band of friends survived on five raisins and a slab of chocolate. These were usually British children, stranded on an island, or lost in a wood, while in the care of an elderly relative, preoccupied with his or her own dark thoughts about the past. Those chocolate bars were thick and sweet, with a slight grainy aftertaste; too sweet, to her taste, now: Cadbury bars. She was not a child who particularly liked the woods, or camping, or the damp. What she liked was the idea of being stranded. Now, when her children hunt in her handbag for sweets, they are usually rewarded. At the theater, when she handed her ticket to the attendant, who knows her by sight, she was glad to see that the movie she planned to see (sometimes, when the film bores her, she slips into another screening room and watches a different film from the middle, and then stays until it starts again) was close to the ladies' room. After buying her cup of tea, Caroline went into the ladies' room and sat on the leather bench to listen to the message. There is a mirror across from the bench. Caroline has looked at herself in that mirror perhaps one hundred times or more, holding the hand of a small child, wearing a leather bomber jacket, a quilted coat, a raincoat, fixing her lipstick before going back out to meet her husband before they go out to dinner after the movie, or go home and pay the babysitter. It is not snowing in the mirror; by now, it is late April or May, five years after the freezing cold evening in Minneapolis. It is twelve days before Alastair's birthday.

Caroline is thinking about Etta Place. Now there is very little Caroline does not talk about, except she does not talk about
you. Which is too bad. No, it is not. And she does not talk
about Alastair, or at least not much. She will say, The boy I was
living with after college. Then she thought that increments were
important: a little bite of a sandwich could lead later to another
bite of a sandwich, she would take her toe out of the water and
stop waiting; waiting for Charon to call, to sweep her up, and
instead she would let him pass by without exchanging a word,
without asking for a cigarette, without asking, *Avete il tempo?*
Charon always knows what time it is; he always has time. *He
makes time.* A child who thinks that if she closes her eyes, she is
invisible. I have to stitch this together quickly, before the bark-
ing dog wakes us from sleep. If one dream replaces another, is
it the same dream? It does not have to be. That is what we will
see. But remember when the pear is ripe, it will fall from the
tree by itself. Caroline believed in one bite and then another.
And she is telling you, a small boy hiding sweets in his pockets
because he is mean, to be quiet. *Caroline and Caroline, Caroline
and Alastair, Alastair and Alastair*: by telling a story you are trying to wake yourself up. But he was still there, at the moment
she woke. Yes, and we do not know anything about how that
turned out, really, do we—he might have been an ass.

Then whose call was she waiting for? Yours—she is waiting
for you to call. But the trick is to stay on Caroline. To keep her
from faltering. That evening in January 2008, when Caroline
did not call Alastair from the phone in the hotel room where
it was snowing, placing a call to another place—Maine—where it
was certainly also snowing, or had just snowed, or was about to
snow; she had seen Alastair precisely once in twenty-three years,

three months before, the night in the house, drinking Lagavulin and eating sausages by the fire smoking in the grate. What did Caroline want? As a child she had been fascinated by the stories of mystics who could walk on burning coals. She has feet with high arches; from certain angles her feet look deformed. Her heel fits perfectly into the arch of her foot. At eleven, her youngest daughter looks like a princess who has been put under a spell and turned into a cat. When she is home, she does not like to leave Caroline's side. She reads *The Hobbit* in Caroline's bed, her T-shirt riding up over her snowman leggings. A few weeks ago, while Caroline was reading the newspaper beside her, she noticed her daughter's hip, the iliac wing arching from her pelvis, like a bird bone below the surface of her skin, and her mind spun to a moment twenty-five years ago; she was a few weeks past twenty, stirring on the sofa in an apartment on Horatio Street where Alastair lived with his tall girlfriend. It was very early in the morning, the honeyed light just speckling the bamboo blinds. She pretended she was asleep. Later—they were living together, he kept disappearing, coming back with his arms full of lilacs, penniless, in the middle of the night or early in the morning—he held her hip as if to pull it out of its socket, saying, "Fuck, just grow up, you have to," as if he could wrench his fingers under that bone and make a wish.

> And he made a little fiddle of her breastbone
> Oh, the wind and rain
> The sound could melt a heart of stone
> Cryin' oh the dreadful wind and rain

An electric plant pulsing in a hidden forest. A bird's-eye view. A girl drawn by a Spirograph needle: a waste of time. By the time Caroline did or did not call Alastair from the hotel in Minneapolis where it was snowing in the mirror, a forest had grown up between them. By the time Caroline landed in the kitchen of the house with the painted willow at Christmas, her bony arm held by a crone, she and Alastair had been together, on and off, for two years, with much shouting and recrimination, and Caroline feeling her heart lurch in her throat, and imagining throwing herself off the parapet of the small apartment which she and Alastair shared on West Eighty-Fourth Street, where she picked at the wallpaper with her fingernail until it tore, revealing silver paper underneath.

Shall I tell it the way you would tell a story? You would say: When I first came to New York from Turin, I had a love affair with a woman I met on a bus. Caroline did not meet Alastair on a bus. When you tell stories, you say: It was complicated, but it lasted only a brief time. For Caroline, it was complicated, and it went on and on, in a forest under the sticks and leaves, in a grove of locust trees where a lost penknife is buried under the cold earth. Alastair wrote to Caroline, decades later, that what confounded him the most was her kindness. Caroline is done, she thinks, with being kind. There are two Carolines, the Caroline who understands what is said to her, and the one who understands but rends her garments nonetheless: the Caroline who understands making your bed and lying in it, and the Caroline who lies in her bed and has bad dreams, many of which she has made for herself, cutting them out with nail scissors. When her children were small and woke with nightmares, she would go to them and put out her hand and say, "Give it to me," and she would put it away in her pocket. There is no one to whom she can hand over her dreams. Now her children tell her to sit down, she is circling the kitchen incessantly, taking out a loaf of bread, putting it away. They can't talk to her when she is moving. When she begins a story, they roll their eyes and ask, "Is there a point to this?" Five minutes in—Caroline has sat down, she has picked up her cup of cold coffee, they say, "You've told us already"; they do not know yet that the stories that are repeated are the important ones, that the point of the story is that it is repeated, that inside the story is a fairy tale, a walnut shell, a tiny boat, a tin can; she says, "I will tell you the end first." Because the beginning is the same as any beginning.

Leaves are starting to fall from the locusts. Soon it will be winter. I will return to the city and walk across the park by the bandstand. I will drive back and forth in the snow, like the girl in the story. But what has happened to Gerda? Have you left her in the snow? No, that story ends. Gerda finds Kai, and the shard which has lodged in his heart melts, and they go back to their house—it is her house now, time has passed, her grandmother is dead. The stars in the sky over the town square, where Kai first heard the sleigh bell, are sharp in the cold air. But Caroline? She is the boy who makes glass sculptures that fill with light; she is the woman stubbing out a cigarette, pouring water over cold coffee grounds; the ring of sleigh bells is the sound the triangle makes when struck, for in the end it is impossible for her not to have one foot out the door; the diamond of light from the half-open door shears the dark. Is she Kai, not Gerda? Caroline has so wanted to be the one who loves. Good. Now can you get me a glass of water when I ask you, hmm?

I'd rather skip that scene, if you don't mind. I know what this feels like, and it has your name on it. A month after Caroline met

Alastair in Maine, driving down the long whitened alley of
trees, the birches blistered with snow, she had found herself
weeping in the car on a small highway in Connecticut, and
pulled off onto the shoulder. But this—besetting, she calls it
to herself, as if a great taloned bird had snatched her up—she
knows now isn't Alastair's, but hers: it is a moment that has
been pushed too far, and she has pushed it, because as it goes
over the cliff she can step aside and watch it fall, as when the
bird lets go and his prey smashes into a quarry's long slit, its
marbled vein strewn with broken branches. She can step aside,
entranced; as it goes over she can watch, as if from a long distance, as it ricochets down time's alley, and behind her a little
door opens to a room that does not change, a small carry cot,
a felt squirrel, a toy telephone painted blue, an old box phone
from a toy phone booth. "Who is calling?" she asks, when it
rings. When she's upset, she pulls at her hands. Each hand pulls
at the other as if trying to pull her fingers out of the sockets one
by one. When Caroline was very small, and later, too, her father
sang to her. He liked to sing. At first there were songs. All the
songs were little stories. Standing on the edge Caroline sang
bits of those songs to herself, over and over, little chants: *me
and Mamie O'Rourke, in Dublin's fair city, he promised to buy me a
bunch of blue ribbons, the old gray goose is dead.* The songs trav-
eled far inside her, ferrying cargo, little boats on the rivers that
were Caroline. Ferrying cargo. When she is upset, she pulls at
her hands. It is an involuntary gesture, her fingers catching on
her rings. Only once it is set in motion, hurtling forward, only
then can she say, *Stop.*

I'd rather skip that scene, if you don't mind. When Caroline
watched that movie, she was waiting in the back of the theater

for you to call. She will not do that again; she is older and wiser.
(But she does, she does.) She will take herself in hand. But
what was Caroline waiting for in the park? Did he call? Yes. He
was in love with someone else by then, a girl who worked in a
coffee shop. He left his wife. Caroline went to see him; he was
living in a rundown apartment in Orono, above a thrift shop.
Then he was in love with Caroline again. *I have never stopped
loving you*, he wrote, a month ago. Then he called to say that
he had decided to get married again, to a woman he met at the
library. Caroline went to the wedding. Did she go? Not yet. Soon
it will be snowing. The dog will sleep on the hearthrug, she will
not be able to see the hand in front of her face. But it is better,
you said, to see from a long way off. Yes. Do you remember the
word for hearth, in the poem by Montale? *Il focolare*. You did not
remember it, you had to look it up. Why are you talking with
my voice in your mouth? Because I am waiting to see you, to see
what happens—I began to tell you about Caroline so I would
have something to show for it. To show for what? For heartbreak.
It was a story invented to tell you. It was to last for one hundred
days. Perhaps it is best, you know, not to be so sure about things.

*

Here is one end. In August of 1985, Alastair interviewed Siad
Barre for the national radio program for which he was a reporter. Did Alastair go to Mogadishu for an interview with Siad
Barre, or did he interview him in New York? The interview,
wherever it was, lasted seven hours. By the middle of the interview, Alastair had fallen in love with him. Or he fell in love
with the cause of the people, with the idea of the new stadium

in Mogadishu, with the slogan "No one can prevent the sunshine from reaching us." It doesn't matter what he had fallen in love with; by the end of the day he had decided to move to Somalia. He assembled stringer jobs for various publications and flew to Somalia after Christmas. He came back a month later. He wanted to move to Africa, and he wanted Caroline to come with him. She refused. She liked her job, at an agency that tried to save buildings of historical interest, and where she spent her days researching and writing and sometimes paying a visit to a falling-down church, or a building that had housed the studio of a well-known, if sadly forgotten, painter or sculptor. She was tired of being in love with Alastair. Even when he was home, he would disappear for days on end, or, instead, never leave the apartment. Then he would skip work and spend all day drinking: *I can offer you only: this world like a knife. I am so wise I had my mouth sewn shut.*

To divert herself, she entertained the attentions of someone who was much nicer than Alastair. This was Peter, who wrote for the metro desk of *The New York Times*, and spent a good deal of time interviewing cops and members of the city council. It depressed him that, week after week, year after year, the same things spun out of control in the same ways, but he maintained an attitude of cheerful resignation. Every couple of weeks in the Blue Bar at the Algonquin he asked her to marry him. On Wednesdays and sometimes on Fridays, she went downtown to meet a Czech poet, who liked to take her to an Indian restaurant near his apartment on Bethune Street, and to play chess after they made love, usually very quickly. He always won the game, equally quickly. Sometimes he took her to parties. He was, to

Caroline then, very old; Caroline's grandfather had taught her a few opening moves, but they were transparent. Moves for babies, the poet told her fondly, which is right because you are a baby. When they played she wore his blue velour bathrobe. When he went to his house in the country, which was set back in a vast field, he would call her on the telephone in her office and discuss the blackbirds that came to sit on the fence and look at him through his window; these were the spirits of his parents. *Why not*, thought Caroline.

Caroline did not want to move to Somalia. She wanted to marry Alastair, and in the meantime she wanted to play chess with the poet in his blue bathrobe and be taken out to dinner by Peter. It is not true, exactly, that she wanted to marry Alastair. She wanted to marry a version of Alastair that did not exist, an imaginary, big-hearted Alastair, but instead she loved him, rather than the poet, or Peter, because she could not abide anyone for very long who did not break her heart. These were the days of long-playing vinyl records; one could pick up and put the needle down anywhere. The third time Alastair went to Mogadishu, Caroline refused once again to go with him, and maddened him further by leaving New York to live alone in the little seaside town where she had spent summers as a child.

But now, as Alastair pointed out when they talked intermittently on the telephone over erratic connections, as if the wires themselves were dipped in water and flame, it was winter: winter was a season they spent together. It was hot in Mogadishu, she could leave the cold house, come, and warm herself at his side. Both Caroline and Alastair maintained an allegiance to the places where as children they had spent summers, which was accompanied, in Caroline's case, by punishing rituals: swimming lessons in the cold at dawn, then sailing drills in which she was taught to tack around an orange life jacket thrown into deep water and rescue the drowning life preserver by stopping in front of it "on a dime," a phrase that confused her. In the harbor, the tide was one of the longest in the world, going out ten or twelve feet and then rushing back like a train. A mile farther out was a target ship the navy used for practice at night, and beyond it a vanished island that emerged at low tide. When she was a child this island was a destination on long day sails. In her nightmares, she conflated the target ship and the island. The ship had bombed the island, and that was why it disappeared. It was not too long after the war; such things, she knew, were possible.

"But winter," said Alastair. Instead of going to Mogadishu, Caroline moved into a cold house in the center of the village. The house was haunted by two sisters whose spirits lived on the listing, warped top floor, where the rooms were filled with old iron bedsteads and lamps that would someday be rewired; old lamps with complicated plugs and sockets, old-fashioned, impossible to use. Sometimes in the middle of the night the lights went on and off of their own accord. Later, she would live in an apartment in New York that had been inhabited by three deaf sisters—there was a system of red lightbulbs installed to alert them to the doorbell—and she would think of those lamps. She did not know then—how could she?—that she herself would haunt the house, would return to it twenty-five years later, and her younger self would at first entice and flatter her, then turn on her, a bad child glimpsed in the hall mirror, an elaborate affair topped by leering cherubs, a child savant who has been taught only one or two opening moves.

How could she have known? You are thinking, Anyone with any sense would have known, or would have looked ahead; but that was the person she would have liked to turn out to be. But how? Caroline was an American; her spyglass set her at the center of the universe, beyond which there were still closed-off places: the Iron Curtain, which she pictured, with a scant sense of history, as a metal grate on a dilapidated storefront selling matches and carbolic acid, who knows what, the Kremlin of the future impossible to see, even through a spirit lamp. Who was this person, whom she would have liked to be? Someone who did not have to type "When did the Cold War end?" into what is now called, with quaint precision, as if it were coal-powered, a search engine. The answer: for a moment, then never. Later, when she spent some time in that house, she found a painting by her first husband lodged in the passage between the pantry and the dining room, a rose-and-gold sunset over the inlet where as a child she had rescued the life preserver from drowning. But by now it was a house in a dream; she could not find her way around. When she had lived there, she would swear it, a door had opened into the front room from the kitchen. The door had vanished. The winter she lived in the house the space shuttle *Challenger* took off and exploded in seventy-three seconds, disintegrating over the Atlantic off the coast of Florida, killing everyone aboard. This was before the Internet; nevertheless, sixty-five percent of the American population knew about the disaster within an hour. Caroline told Alastair, who happened to call that morning from a radio phone. When she hung up, she walked through the door to the front room through the door that is not there now, picturing a spume of smoke, and Alastair shirtless rolling a cigarette in a tent where the air stuck to his skin. Next to the door was a collection of cookbooks from the 1970s. When you picked them up, old recipes—Quick Beef Stroganoff, Chicken Timbale, cut from newspaper cooking columns—fell out like brown leaves. Many of the recipes had titles that contained descriptive nouns: Turkey Surprise, Zucchini Fantasia, Peach Bombe. Once the bomb exploded, everything after it looked like a bomb; it was possible, even, to domesticate it, to change it into something else. An island could disappear. The sound of carpets, beating.

"It's winter," said Alastair. The rhythm of their—not love affair—life together was that they stayed together in the winter, and in the summer, flaring up, roused from their long sleep, lighting firecrackers for the noise they made, they parted. She can see now how very close they were to childhood, and that summer, the idea of a long raft of indolent days—for they were Americans—was a habit they could not break. They would separate, as if the demands of their life, which pretended to be the life of two adults, were too taxing. Alastair wrote her long letters on ruled paper in ballpoint pen, in pencil sometimes; there are stains on the letters, as if he had left them out on a table too long. A lit match in a bad mood. He wrote about fire ants and getting and not getting interviews, and the sound of the streets at night, and drinking contraband gin. The Shebelle was the color of tar. It was extremely hot. He had a fever and he was shivering. In the very early spring Caroline moved out of the huge drafty house and into a shack in the woods on a still-iced-over pond. It was extremely cold. She wore two pairs of pants and an old bearskin coat that had belonged to her grandfather. She wore it to sleep. It snowed, and snowed some more. She slept next to a dangerous gas heater that prickled her dreams. At night she could hear the black ice cracking. There was a phone in the shack, and once in a while it rang in the middle of the night. It was Alastair. He was or was not coming back. Because these conversations, punctuated by long silences in which Caroline drifted off to sleep, occurred in the very early hours of the morning in the woods, with the sound of the ice breaking up, when she woke up she was never sure if she had dreamed them—Alastair's voice, wings batting across two oceans, full of reflexive questions, asking if she was awake. In those years transatlantic calls were often bad connections.

"But it is winter," said Alastair. The smoke of the *Challenger* looked like the wake of a boat, a speedboat pulling a waterskier behind it. For the rest of her life when she thinks of the *Challenger*, she will hear Alastair breathing on the phone, and see Christa McAuliffe holding the tow rope, water-skiing in a spiral of smoke, a spiral that curves into the shape snow makes kicked up behind a plow; a moment in which Joseph Cornell sees that the curve of a paper swan's neck mirrors the curve in the open page of a book in a dollhouse, and the arc is radiant, the place where history resides. A place where the lost Minoans speak, a radioactive moment, spawning half-lives. There was no way to know then that the *Challenger*, with its provocative name—with a schoolteacher on board!—would be a trope, a homemade disaster, an adolescent calamity, that prepared the sixty-five percent of Americans who saw it on television within an hour for 9/11, fifteen years later. Challenging what? Caroline thought. What is being challenged? There is no television in the house. Alastair asks, from his hut made of wattles, drinking gin at what in Mogadishu is eight in the morning, slapping mosquitoes, "Do you remember the day we went sledding?" "Hold on tight," says Caroline. On the phone Alastair starts to cry. She is a little bit pleased by this, her ability to make him cry over ten thousand miles of telephone wires. Because it is extremely cold, she is wrapped in a red-and-black wool blanket and is wearing shearling slippers that Alastair bought her as a kind of joke for Christmas. The shearling slippers look like hooves, and she thinks of Mr. Tumnus in Narnia, the faun in the forest. "Come back," she says to Alastair, who is now weeping into the phone. The line goes dead. Caroline tries calling back, dialing the long spiral of numbers Alastair has given her, but cannot produce a ring. Their favorite movie was *Les enfants du paradis*. A movie that many years later she took her younger daughter to see, who found it so boring they had to leave. For Caroline, being suspended in time is everything. *"Vous aviez raison, Garance. C'est tellement simple, l'amour."* It is not everything. Say what happened. What happened? She felt like the girl in the plane wreck in *Flying Down to Rio* who has to leave the island hideaway in the middle of the picture because she has lost her nerve. *"Je meurs du silence, comme d'autres meurent de la faim et de la soif."*

*

You are not telling me, exactly; it is like trying to pin down a butterfly. I gave you those two butterflies, they hang now by the side of your bed like a crucifix. Once upon a time there was a boy whose parents loved him but did not pay him very much attention. Which boy? Was that me? It is you, and it is Alastair.

My family was different. This is a Caroline story, about Alastair, full of ice. Remind me about the Ice Age. This is not the Ice Age.

It is pinning down a butterfly. The line Alastair liked from *The Ice Storm*—Caroline had to look it up—was "the past was so past it hurts." Better, yes, to forget it—the remark of a person, quite young, feeling sorry for himself. It was the middle of winter. When Caroline thinks about Alastair it is always freezing. In the past twenty-eight years, she has seen him once in the summer, in the middle of the night, deep in the country. Otherwise, ice crystals form when she thinks of him, lines etched with a diamond on frozen glass. A year, or less, before he went to Mogadishu—she cannot remember—he had been reporting a story, and for one reason or another had to hole up in a hotel in Wilmington, after a ship called the *Grand Eagle* spilled thousands of gallons of oil into the Delaware River, near Marcus Hook.

She had taken the train to stay with him at the Hilton, where his clothes were strewn around the room and where, it turned out, he had been making paper airplanes of transcripts sent to the press—a room in a hotel in Mexico City, where they stayed, decades later, looked exactly the same—and he had met her on the platform. It was so cold their breath rose in clouds. She stepped from the train into his arms. This was thirty years ago. There was a smudge on the collar of his down parka, and he smelled of Drum tobacco. It was years before she could lift her eyes from the cashier at any bodega to the rows of cigarettes behind the register, the dark blue eye of the cellophane package: Halfzware shag. She stepped from the open door of the train into his arms, the cigarette he had discarded when the doors opened a lit sparkler on the platform, as if he himself was a bomb about to go off. A man from the Salvation Army was jangling bells in the lay-by. *Once in royal David's city* . . .

When Kai looked up from his sled in the town square, the bells called to him, come away.

When Caroline stepped into Alastair's arms on the platform, it was the last time in her life she would feel at home. Folly. As Etta says, "I'd rather skip that scene, if you don't mind." Which scene would Caroline skip? For years afterward, she would dream that she was changing trains in the winter, watching the snowy landscape shoot by. According to her ticket, she would have to change trains in Odense. But either the platform disappeared under her feet when she disembarked, or she watched herself through the window, her head in a book, on a train heading in the opposite direction.

The first time she went to bed with Alastair, in September 1982, it was the middle of the night and the lights were off. The lights were off? You like the lights on, a little. I didn't know then what I liked! They had been talking in the dark on the terrace, which was then just tar paper and broken glass, and smoking and drinking gin. The first time Caroline went to bed with Alastair the lights were on. It was the middle of the night, in New York, September 1982. She had not planned on it. They were friends. He had once, furtively, undressed her in the very early morning in the summer three years ago, teasing her T-shirt above her breasts while she pretended to sleep, but for Caroline it was as if she had dreamed that, and the vision, which sometimes held its wings over her when she waited with other friends, for Alastair to meet them at the movies, or after class, where he was always in the middle of lighting a cigarette against the wind, cupping his hands for the spirit flame, was like a cloud in the corner of her eye, a cinder. It was very late and he said, "If I do not leave now then we will go to bed," and she did not think for a moment, No. In the half-light, she could feel his back as he moved over her; it was corrugated, like cardboard, or tree bark. She could feel it under her palms. Alastair moved over her and around her, he was insistent. He smelled like Drum tobacco and gin and something else—talcum powder. Caroline was twenty-two and Alastair was twenty-four. She couldn't see or feel anything for certain in the dark but the ridges on his back were like a fish skeleton, like the bones of the tetrapods that came out of the sea and made purchase on dry land. They sang to her, bone on gristle, fish in the pan. A fiddle of her breastbone.

You are always in a hurry, you think nothing will keep. But it keeps. Look how long things keep! Look at Caroline and Alastair! I do not want there to be a story. But there is, *bella*, there is.

His back was corrugated. Under her fingers it felt like corduroy. As a child she had learned the etymology of corduroy: *corde du roi*. When the king made his way over the mud, the carriage track was made level for him by a path of cut logs. Like many explanations, fanciful. She thought of that now as her hands ran over his back. His back felt like the strings of a piano. In the house in which she grew up, outside Boston, there was a huge black, shiny piano called a baby grand. When would it grow up? she wondered. There were keys on the piano as there were keys on a typewriter. Caroline learned how to type on the piano before she began to write on a typewriter; in some ways, they are one and the same to her. The piano bared its shiny white teeth when its long black mouth was propped open. Underneath it smelled dusty and cold. Like the grave, Caroline thought, the words rising unbidden; she had no idea what a grave smelled like. Under her fingers the thick, tightly coiled strings of the piano could be made to vibrate, just slightly. She took lessons, stopped. Sometimes she thinks now she would like to learn how to play again; now she cannot play at all, but for the first bars of one Bach invention her fingers remember. The first time Alastair moved over her, straining against her like a tuning fork, a divining rod looking for water, like a man on a wide expanse of beach looking for coins (his head was buried in her neck, she was wearing a hoop earring that became tangled in her hair), she thought for the first time in years of the feel of the piano strings. What is this? she thought. She had the gift, bestowed on children, of taking things as they came, with no thought of her capacity for agency. She would have been bemused and a little terrified by the idea that Alastair would not rise from her bed for years. Perhaps if she had looked for them when she shut her eyes, pictures would have appeared: Blake's angel of "The Resurrection," a Catherine wheel. And later, from the tarot pack, the Ten of Swords.

As Alastair moved over Caroline, her hands plucked at his back like birds searching furrows for seeds. The only light was from the window which shone a yellow square on the back garden wall. Years afterward, Caroline would befriend an artist who worked with light. He installed a camera in a gallery that projected light coming through a window on a blank wall. But which was the real window? Alastair's hands worked their way into her body until she was a glove turned inside out. There was not much to Caroline. Later Alastair would say he could feel himself inside her on the surface of her skin.

When Alastair and his brother and sister were children, in Maine each summer, they played freeze tag. Because his brother and sister were younger, they were given big flashlights and Alastair was given what was left, a tiny flashlight of the kind that attached to your key chain, to light up the lock in the dark. They played under the trees—they looked like fireflies, glim-mering, shouting, and whooping. Sometimes they decided to be very quiet, and the light swooped and glittered without a sound. Because he had a little light, it meant that Alastair was invisible.

He was invisible. It was the 1970s, in any case, no one was paying too much attention to children. In the country it was one thing, in the city another. When they returned to the city, and to school and the bus and math homework and getting dark early, Alastair began to walk home from school through Central Park at night with his little penlight, instead of taking the bus. He listened for owls. At the beginning, he would find a bench by the reservoir and sit. No one ran then, it was quiet. If he sensed someone coming near, he would disappear. He liked the idea of flight, the feel of it in the woods. The park became a dark interior place in his heart that belonged to him. There was a girl he liked a little bit. The school he went to was all boys, but he knew some girls, sisters or friends of friends. She had a cloud of light hair, like a dandelion. Later she joined a band. Caroline knew her a bit, she went to school with her brother, but for years she was a nymph in Alastair's dreams. But girls, even this one, came later. He moved like a cat, like a boy with a secret. He tested the seams of the world that enveloped him, coming home late and then a little later, saying he was doing his homework at a friend's apartment, a science project. They were working on something about batteries, something about tree sap. He had to remember what the project was. At the same time, in Sudbury, Caroline was being picked up by a boy at the bus stop and driven to school. He was a few years older than she was, and he drove carefully, quickly. The car was expensive. She sat way over by the window. She didn't like him, not particularly; what she liked was lying. She liked saying she was in one place when she was in another. It was her first inkling of privacy. Alastair spent the hours after school sidling among the trees. It got dark early. Soon it was dark and the cold came in, a train shifting its gears and blowing clouds of steam that froze in midair. He had lost his pocket light at the end of September, but it didn't matter. He moved like a shadow in the trees. He wore his school backpack like a coat of arms. Sometimes there were leaves or bark in his hair when he returned home. His parents were often out.

His sister noticed the leaves in his hair, and after that he checked his reflection in the elevator mirror. At school there was a field trip. His French class was taken to a movie theater, to see *L'enfant sauvage*. A boy, naked, found in the woods, hunted down by a pack. The year was 1798. It was a true story. Alastair experimented with not speaking. His father spoke sharply to him. Alastair wrote on a piece of paper: *It's an experiment for school, for French class.* This was a little mixed up, but his father bought it. What do French people say, his brother asked, *rien?* Snickering. When Caroline was a child, she talked so much without stopping that on long car trips her father said he would give her a nickel for every five minutes she did not speak. She learned to stop talking. Silence went with the smell of black Naugahyde, the thick window in the back seat rolled halfway down, the window lacy with pollen.

School came easily to him. He understood that as long as he did well in school, he could do what he liked. Later, when he lived in the woods and sat in the car outside the local stadium because the soccer field was freezing and called Caroline on the phone, he still understood that, but by now the days were difficult to manage. He wrote a long story in French about a boy and girl who were in love but were parted by her wicked uncle, who wanted the girl to himself. He thought about the girl with dandelion hair. By then it was snowing.

By then it was snowing. Many years later, one winter in New York, it was snowing in the park. It had snowed for days. The statue of Balto, the rescue dog, north of the zoo, was covered in snow, and the beautiful birds had been taken in from the aviary. The bears on the clock, which Caroline had loved as a child and which had recently been repaired, had snow on their fur, like the Bremen Town musicians, brought here to spin the hours. She had learned to tell time on that clock, sitting on the bench with her grandfather, her paw in his. Just then, by what became Strawberry Fields, Alastair in his school sweater was throwing a ball to his father. Thwack.

*

Here are Gerda and Kai sitting together. They are older now, they live in their two houses, over the town square, and they have broken through the wall, so now it is one house, large and airy and full of sunlight. The roses grow over the door. Gerda's grandmother has died. Their own children are grown up. They walk to the edge of the wood in the evening, past the lake that was once frozen over. Now that it is warmer, it doesn't often freeze in the winter. Blackberries grow around the lake, and fir trees. The dog walks beside them, his black shadow always a little way ahead. Sometimes they call to her, "Come now." The sky, so close, closer than before, is spliced with sunset, green and pink. Sometimes, when they lie down together, Gerda feels a sudden movement under his skin, a tremor. The marks of the Snow Queen's corset of bells have faded to flickers of moonlight. They speak mainly to each other. It has been this way for a long time. Sometimes, the telephone rings. Long distance, says Gerda to Kai. The mirror above the mantel—*Sul caminetto?* Yes—is freckled with age, but it reflects the light in the room, winter and summer. Kai writes a column for the local newspaper about birds. It is after a plague that beset the world, polluting the air, but now he has heard a nightingale again in the woods, as he did when he was a child. They have returned, along with the swallowtail butterfly, and more creatures, voles and mice, make their homes under the roots of the trees. The octagonal bench in the middle of the square where his sled broke into smithereens was replaced long ago. It is painted green, and every year the town repaints and mends it. As for the sled itself, when their grandchildren visit in winter, they prefer skiing, but the little one likes them to pull her over the snow, in her jacket embroidered with a little bear and a flying bee. Sometimes it is very cold, and icicles hang over the doorway like the teeth of an enormous animal, a mastodon, or a sperm whale, and when she looks out from the maw of the

house, standing in the doorway under the fanlight, she listens
for bells. *I'll skip this scene*, she thinks, *if you don't mind*.

But it is as if it is happening again, this world like a knife,
unfolding in the creases of the Japanese fan, a snow scene,
carefully delineated with figures . . . Caroline, penknife, Kai,
Gerda. "Where have you been since we last met?" said Peer Gynt
to Solveig.

But that's a fairy story, is it not? Tell me, then, something that
is not. The clouds tussled over Belvedere Castle, where, much
later even than that snowy day, we sat at Bethesda Fountain
and you said, *Ci siamo innamorati, ma non sappiamo cosa fare al
riguardo*. You are a schoolgirl, you are always in love, and your
moves are the moves of a child. You need only the blue bathrobe,
to begin quoting Akhmatova. And then the phone rings, and
someone says, "Are you sitting down?" The tangle of wires, red,
blue, orange, violet. And over the wire the sound of an explosion,
quite near, a streak of skywriting, which annihilates itself in a
puff of smoke. But that is better than the quiet, yes?

I have left Caroline and Alastair in the snow, in Central
Park, separated by forty years, she in her fur hat and he with his
penknife. By now, he has another knife. Yes, I can offer you only:
this world like a knife; that is actually what he said. It was true.
But it was not his to offer. A gift is not usually something the
beloved already has. And what was it? The lizard of fear. The
boy notching the root of the locust, the frozen pond, with its
wreath of rowan leaves. Just yesterday—the day I came with
the flowers?—yes, the day you came with the flowers, Caroline
received a note from Alastair. What did the note say? He wrote

that he thought of her constantly, it was the season they could never get through, summer. Why was that? Stop, stop asking. Why? I think you ask too much and give too little in return. Flowers. Flowers are not everything. I think it was because they would have to come out of the cold. They would have had to give up grief. Let me get back to them, standing in the same place forty years apart, by the ball fields, like figures in a pantomime. No. Leave them be.

When she got out of the car and began to walk down the lane to the barn (there were many cars; it was not the wrong time, nor the wrong day), she saw Alastair immediately, a swab of whitewash against the grass, but he did not see her. There was a small girl with a pink crinoline skirt and a man with dreadlocks down his back, intricately plaited, like a Japanese bamboo basket. He bent over the little girl. The white irises were beautiful this year, a flotilla of moths by the pond, and there were Maria and Otto. Together they exclaimed over the irises. "I got lost!" she said. Otto looked at her quizzically. "I was just thinking of a thousand things," she said. "You can go straight to Halifax that way," said Maria, "I did once." Maria, Alastair's mother, her hair white now. They paused to consider this. I will forget, she thought. As a wedding present she had bought a red-glazed plate with a picture of a bird. It was something she herself would have liked to have, something she knew they had no use for. When she went into the barn, she smelled pine and water and tar soap, and heard the rushing water. She climbed the stairs to the loft and rested her forehead on the mirror. There. There you are, she thought, as if the glass remembered her—this mirror in particular, standing on the maple bureau—did not as much see as remember. The whole shebang, she thought. From the top of the stair she could see herself at twenty, reading on the sofa, her fingers on the pleat of the pillow. Then she cared, when he turned on her. You are annihilating me, he said. I am not what you make me out to be. She thought, I never was, the thought a monarch wing. They were to stand by the pond for the ceremony—but it was wet. Then Otto at the foot of the stairs. He had smoked her out. A five-minute warning. Five years ago, it was June and at midnight she had stood with Alastair in the afterlife, knee-deep in the black pond among the white irises, the minnows sucking the stones, stars raining down. She had unsnarled a hammock and hung it between the trees. Thirty years ago, they had walked in the deep snow, the road a figure eight, and under the covered bridge. Now she stood with his mother, Maria, who had never liked her, against the fence where it was dry. She could not hear what he was saying, his mouth moving. Something about love. She remembered the sound of his lips, brushing the telephone. The little girl in the pink crinoline was spinning, her skirt straight out, a pinwheel in a patch of sun. Where could he have gotten that suit? "There's a decent tailor in Portland," said Otto, "Jesus." She had known him since he was a boy. She adjusted her hat. Beyond his shoulder she could see a cap of blond hair and a smear of rose silk, but she could not see her face. She had been mad with grief, but now she was not. She had trapped the butterfly, its printed orange wings; she had fed a name into the fire. Shade fell from the poplars onto the irises. She could feel the breeze gathering. She looked past the barn to the stones with the water rushing over them. I will not sit there again, she thought. The leaves were lit gold in the hazel wood. Such luck the weather has held. His back was toward her. She made no effort to approach, but sat with Maria and Otto. "After all this time," said Otto. "After all this time."

ACKNOWLEDGMENTS

Thanks are due to Pierre Alexandre de Looz, Edwin Frank, Jane Mendelsohn, Leanne Shapton, and Susan Wiviott, for reading and rereading, and for conversation; to Jonathan Galassi, and to Katharine Liptak, at Farrar, Straus and Giroux; to Sarah Chalfant and Luke Ingram at the Wylie Agency, whose abiding interest turned these pages into a book.

Permissions Acknowledgments